NORTHERN LIGHTS

RUBEN ISIAH WILLIAMS

CONTENTS

Nine

Ten

Eleven

Preface

Northern Lights was written with the intention of freeing not only Black boys and girls, but anyone who suffers from anxiety, depression, racism, and abuse. There are so many people who suffer silently with these issues and still try to live normal lives. They go to school and have a great group of friends and they have interesting social lives. Yet, when they return home, they are downed with pressure and life's issues. I want to let you know that regardless of your skin color, gender, or belief, do not give up. Your future depends on how well you power through your experiences. You are here for a reason and, in time, your purpose will come out of hiding and make itself known to you.

This book is dedicated to my wife and children. My wife has always been the rock I needed in all seasons of my life. She pushes me to be greater every day, and I owe my drive to her. My children are my 'why.' I want to be the example that they can see and realize it doesn't matter how you start, but it's how you finish. The hand I was dealt was a card short, but God gave me an ace in the hole. I want to show them that they can be who they are and not be ashamed of their gifts. Be unapologetically YOU!

CHAPTER ONE

The Accident

November 30th Loc'ed Up

Hair is a gift that comes in all shapes and sizes. Straight, curly, stringy, and nappy. It falls and rises, it's puffy, it's shaggy. My hair is more than my definition. It's more than a culture. It influences and it's passed down to generations that are sculpted. The way that I lock it up is not like the cages. It hangs down and out like the black arms in the bars of the institutions that made us. I don't understand why my hair is so dangerous. I can't graduate because of a policy that wants to change us. They've been trying to change us since the beginning of this land. And our hair to our roots is what keeps us grounded more than our washed-up ancestors in the sand. That's why I stay loc'ed up til the day I die. I want my hair to be loc'ed up, not the thoughts in my mind. But I can't leave this state, and they want to cut off the very thing that binds.

I sat in my room cringing while I heard the screeching laugh of B playing cards with her boyfriend and their friends. B became my foster parent when I was 10, and she has given me hell ever since. It was 2:00 in the morning, and I had to be at school at 8:00. They kept me up with cigarette smoke, loud 70s music, and the clanging of the beer bottles every Wednesday. B always came home from bingo at 11:00 and invited the local drunks over to play cards. I swear all they did was drink until they started fighting over someone trying to cheat them out of their money. I would shut the basement room door and try to keep the noise and stench from seeping into the room.

A cloud of cigarette smoke filled the house, but I felt as if there was a cloud that followed me wherever I went. Not of smoke, but of anger, pain, and disappointment. As hard as I tried to move from under the cloud, it always overshadowed me. Since I could remember, I've never had the chance to have a normal childhood. My mother resorted to drug addiction shortly after I was born because she couldn't handle the stress of having a child so young. I constantly glared at old pictures of how beautiful she looked before I came into the picture. She had shiny, curly black hair, smooth fair skin, big, beautiful hazel eyes, and a smile that was to die for. She looked like she could have been a model. But, because of my birthday, I made her ugly. It was my fault she turned to drugs. If I was never born, my mother would still be beautiful and alive.

It seemed as if everything was my fault, and B made it her business to remind me. I constantly had to hear her cackling, southern accent saying,

"You 'gone be just like your sorry daddy. Always messing something up. Look at you, just a mess. The only thing good that comes from you is you living here so I can get this check from the people. Other than that, you killed your mama by driving her to drugs and got your daddy in jail for trying to take care of your sorry behind."

She made me sick with how she talked to me. I always thought once I got out of high school I was going to go far away from B and the ghetto. Sometimes I imagined myself killing B very slowly. I saw myself wrapping my hand around her sweaty neck and watching her eyes turn bloodshot red. Her pasty face would turn blue, then purple. I felt her throat jerking in my hands as she gasped for a puff of air. Her eyes rolled in the back of her head while her neck becomes limp.

But who was I kidding? The stuffed bear I held couldn't feel my disdain towards B. I would never get that opportunity. The best I could say is I hate you in my mind. Besides, she was the closest thing to family I had left.

I lay down on the dingy twin mattress and stared at the ceiling of the basement. It was dim and damp. Spider webs and dust hampered the wood beams on the ceiling. The dark gray metal pipes hang together with string so that they won't leak water, and the concrete floor was hard and cold. This was my living space. I imagined living in a brand-new home where there was grass and a back yard instead of dirt and an alley. There would be kids outside playing with one another instead of fighting and shooting. The only thing on the curb of each house would be basketball hoops, bubbles, bikes, scooters, and children's toys instead of needles, used condoms, shell casings, and yellow police tape.

The house I would live in would have a big kitchen with a see-through refrigerator filled with fruit, milk, juice, and real food. I would press a button on the fridge and music would play my morning playlist while I ate my favorite breakfast: crispy bacon, sausage, scrambled eggs, lightly toasted bagels, and a tall glass of orange juice with ice; instead of a lukewarm fridge with three-day-old pizza and a roach that made its residence in the vegetable tray. I would walk around barefoot on the carpet and the heated, hardwood floors instead of walking around with shoes on because of fear of stepping on a nail or broken glass. To my fortune, none of those things were in my reach. It was a pipe dream. As I closed my eyes, the complete darkness seemed better than the murky reality I had to walk through every day in that house. Sometimes dreams are only mirages, especially when you are thirsty for something else.

"James!" B yelled at the top of the basement steps, "Didn't I tell you to take out this garbage?"

As I laid in bed, I sighed under my breath because it was 2:30, and I should have been asleep by this time, so I already knew what was next. I replied,

"I took it out before I got home from school earlier. I told you that it's your pie smelling like that, and you said you would take care of it."

The pie in the refrigerator was two weeks old. The fridge was already warm, and it never kept anything cold. The only part that worked was the freezer.

"Well, I knew that. I was making sure you did what I told you to do. Anyways, get your tail ready for school because you're about to be late."

B was drunk and had lost track of time. She continued with her yelling and berating me. I had enough. Normally I was quiet and submissive because I hated conflict and it scared me, but for some reason after five years of constant mental and emotional abuse, that was the last straw. I felt anger rise in me that I couldn't control. My emotions and my reaction were always in my control because that was the only thing I could maintain, but my inner self had its own plan this time.

"B, its 2:30 and I was almost sleep before you yelled down here about some stupid garbage. What do you care about my education anyways? You don't take me to school, you don't come to any parent-teacher conferences, or worry about my well-being in general. All you care about is your alcohol, cigarettes, and your crippled boyfriend you got rolling behind you. You need to get your life together and go to rehab or something. You're a fat alcoholic who needs to get a real job instead of collecting a disability check and use foster kids as income. Nobody loves you, and you project that on me. I don't care about you and I never did. Fuck you bitch, I hope you die."

Before I could get the last word out of my mouth, I saw her tumble down the stairs as if someone pushed her with brute force. Her neck snapped forward and her forehead hit the fourth step, her leg got caught underneath her body, and her skin was snagged on a nail on the eighth step. Her body laid still with her bruised face on the thirteenth step and her bloody and broken leg at the bottom step.

I went and stood over her body and saw her gazing at the ceiling. The water from the pipes dripped slowly onto her forehead and rolled down to her nose and into her neck like a baby feeding from a bottle.

Helpless.

She was like a child and I was the only person that could help her. I looked at her chest to see if she was still breathing. To my dismay I saw her breast slightly raising and lowering. The music upstairs was so loud that B's friends didn't hear her fall as they were leaving. At that point I was in a battle internally in which I had to decide—leave B there for dead or call 911.

Leaving B for dead could give me my freedom. I could continue to let her suffer here and die on the steps while I went on as long as I could until somebody started asking questions. I could make up a lie and say I ran away and haven't been home for weeks or months. Or I could 911 and she would recover, and I would go back to my old miserable life with B for four more years. These thoughts put me in a situation I would have never imagined. Out of all the emotions that I thought I'd have in a moment like this, the most prevalent was being emotionless. I felt absolutely nothing. No remorse, excitement, sadness, joy, nothing. My emotion was as empty as her heart. I've dealt with B on such a level for so long that I had become her. I replayed her fall in my mind and I saw her as myself: lifeless, hopeless, and at the mercy of a monster. We switched places.

December 3rd Snapped.

Snapped. (Snaps one finger lightly)

Not my fingers but my words. Prison sentenced in my own home, not the building but my mind.

Snapped. (Snaps one finger louder)

With my fingers I make a loud sound. I can feel the tension be-tween my fingers even though there's blood in between the middle and the thumb (raises up middle finger and thumb). Not a cut, but tears from my eyes. Sometimes I feel led to stay quiet in wraps, while my mind wanders to escape from crap out in the next room. Words can be a gamble. Quick, easy, and to the point. Either hit or miss. Either way when you're done...

Snapped. (Snaps both fingers twice loudly)

...

I have always had a love hate relationship with school. I hated it because I didn't like talking to people I didn't know. On the other hand, I loved it because it was a chance for me to get out of the house and I could hang out with my best friend Gary. I've known him since the sixth grade. We called him Scoop because he was so small that people bigger than him would be able to pick him up with ease. His parents were great people. His mom was a nurse, and his dad was a police officer. His mom would twist my locs for me to keep them fresh. They even paid for my phone so I could be on their plan. Since my house was always filthy and dirty, I showered and washed my clothes at their house. They knew that I wasn't being taken care of properly, so they were like my parents too. Scoop looked out for me when I first met him in middle school because I smelled horrible. His parents had him at a young age just like my parents, so I guess that's why we clicked so easily. We went to a private school, where it was diverse. To go to South Shore, you needed to pay the tuition or get sponsored. The foster care agency I was a part of sponsored two kids every four years. I don't know why they picked me. I guess it was luck of the draw.

The school was huge. It looked as if it was a school right out of the movies. Vaulted ceilings, clean floors, mascot running around every day, and healthy lunches. School was my get away, like a sanctuary where I could feel like every other kid. I loved being able to learn what I didn't know. One of my favorite classes was any type of history. Learning about what happened years before and how culture changed was always interesting to me. In class, one thing I never did was answer questions. I always thought I wasn't smart enough to get them right, but on the tests, I would get A's and B's. I hated speaking in front of a group of people because I didn't talk like all the other Black people. I knew the slang and understood the code, but I wanted to talk like how I wrote. Besides, my hands would clam up, I would start sweating, and my words wouldn't come out. It was best that I stayed quiet.

The thing that I loved doing other than learning was writing. I started writing in my notebook when I noticed B was treating me bad. Everywhere I went, I kept my notebook on me, so if I ever needed to write something down I could. Growing up in the hood was not somewhere you could be proud of writing unless you were a rapper. I've been called nerd, geek, and lame, but I never thought it was cool to be stupid. At any moment, your life is on the line where I lived. I had to learn and observe to survive.

Scoop and I would meet by the bus stop at the corner from our houses. We lived on the same street just four houses down from each other. He was always running late because he over-slept every day. So, while I would wait at the bus stop, I would see him full on sprinting down the street waving me down, signaling me to have the bus driver wait. One day, a few months after the accident, everything started normally until I got on the bus.

"Hey, can you wait for…" As I was showing the bus driver my bus pass, the driver quickly interrupted me. I noticed that the driver was not our regular.

"I see scoop running as fast as he can. I will wait for him," the bus driver said, laughing.

With a confused look on my face I asked,

"How did you know that was Scoop?"

"Shane told me this morning. He's taking my route today because this is the quick route, and I have to be done earlier than he does."

The school had bought some old city busses and renovated them. The bus drivers were hired by the city, but there were designated drivers for our route to the school. Shane was the coolest bus driver ever. Sometimes when I would forget my bus pass, he would let me get on without it. He said I could bring a friend on the bus whenever I wanted without them paying. The best thing he would do is drop us off right in front of my house because we were the last stop to drop off and first stop to pick up in the morning.

As scoop ran on the bus, I made my way to our spot right in the middle next to the door. In the wintertime, the heat would blast right there, and, in the summertime, the air would blow out the coldest. I looked at our seats, and there was a kid sitting there. He had on the Retro 5 Jordan's that came out three days before, black jeans, a black t-shirt, with an all-black Jordan back-pack. To top it off, he had on the brightest gold chain that I'd ever seen. I thought to myself that he must be a new kid going to Tech because we had to wear uniforms at South Shore. It was odd that he was on the bus before us because we're the first stop. I turned around and proceeded to the front of the bus to meet Scoop to tell him we needed to switch seats.

"J, who is the new bus lady? I thought she was going to be pressing me about my bus pass, but she was cool. I told her Shane lets me and you get on sometimes when we forget it at home."

"I don't know who she is, but Shane switched routes with her because she has to leave early or something. Anyways, we gotta sit somewhere else because some guy is sitting in our spot."

Scoop developed a confused look on his face and said,

"How? We're the first people on this bus every day, how is there somebody here before us? Let's go tell him to move."

Scoop and I have different personalities. For him to be the smallest person in our graduating class, he was always the one that loved to fight and start trouble. Me on the other hand, I hated confrontation, but if I ever had gotten to the point of explosion, I wouldn't be able to control it. I guess that's why B had her accident. She was shocked I actually said something to her.

I took a deep breath and said, "Let's just stay in the front. It's way too early to be getting all crazy right now. Besides, this might be his only time on the bus anyway. He could be that lady's son or nephew."

"He better not be here tomorrow because I'll go right over there and tell him to get up before I move him." Scoop said while trying to make his voice deeper. "Niggas don't know that I may be little, but I can fight. The only thing people will try to do to me is pick me up and slam me because I'm little. Let me hit my growth spurt then it's over. I'm a young Mike Tyson in the making. Gary 'Scoop' Rockland III baby! I'm up next. I'm already at that boxing gym over by the park getting trained by Uncle P. He taught me where to hit people to knock them out with one punch and everything. He used to be a professional boxer until he got into a car accident that almost killed him."

"First of all, you're not Mike, second, I can beat you up with my left hand, and third of all I didn't know Uncle P used to box. I saw pictures of him of how big he used to be. His daughter goes to Tech over on the Northside."

Uncle P was the neighborhood OG. He kept all the kids in the neighborhood in check if he caught them doing something stupid. Unc started selling drugs after he recovered from his accident. He went to prison for ten years for getting caught with dope. Word around the neighborhood was somebody snitched on him. They couldn't get him with everything, that's why he only served ten years.

"You need to calm down man. It is 7:15 in the morning, and you already talking about fighting. You got issues, bro."

"Yeah, whatever you say," Scoop said with a smirk on his face. "Now I know you don't like talking about this because you never told me what all happened, but how is B doing?" Scoop asked concerned. "How long has it been since the fall? Two months?"

I rolled my eyes and answered reluctantly, "Yeah it's been about two months."

Scoop asked, "So are you still taking care of her? How long did the doctor say it was going to take for her to fully recover?"

"Eight to twelve months."

"I know that sucks, but the real question is, how are you? I know you hate that lady, now you have to take care of her. How are you doing that because if I was you, I would be making her life miserable. She wouldn't eat for days; she wouldn't have a bath or anything."

I took a deep breath after a short pause because I didn't want to answer.

"Ok, I really don't like talking about this, so after I tell you this, I am not talking about it again. After she fell, I decided that I would call 911, and they came and got her. I didn't want to call them because of how she treats me, but something in me made me look up and call them. After I called them, I was still calm. I never panicked or got out of control. I saw that she was bleeding so I wiped the blood from her face and her leg. I didn't want to move her from her spot because I wanted them to see exactly how she landed and where she fell. I went upstairs after I cleaned her up a bit to turn off the loud music and grabbed some extra towels just in case. She looked like she was knocked out so I didn't say anything to her. I stayed there sitting on my bed silent as I listened for the sirens outside. They came to the door and asked me how she fell, and I told them she was yelling at

me and—"

Before I could continue Scoop chimed in, "I would have pushed the bitch."

"Scoop! Can I finish telling you what happened before you go into kill mode? Anyways, I told them what I said to her and—"

"I would have I told her—"

"Scoop! Anyways, I told them what I'd said to her right before she fell, and I thought I was going to get in trouble, but I didn't. So, after they put her on the cart, we got in the ambulance and went to the hospital. Now the reason why I take care of her is because as we were riding in the ambulance, she came to and grabbed my hand. She turned to me, tears coming down her face. She looked as if she was thanking me for not letting her die. Once we got the hospital, they ran tests and got her in the bed. The doctor said she hit the back and the front of her head with so much force that she wouldn't be able to talk for a few months and her personality could be different. She's in a wheelchair right now, so she can't even walk. I was going back and forth from the house to the hospital before she was discharged after about three weeks. I called a Lyft for us to get back home. I didn't want to tell anybody because it had been nice and peaceful around the house these past few months. I've been cleaning and buying groceries with her food stamp card and everything. So, life is good right now. I just wish she could stay like this forever."

By the time I finished the story, Scoop was astonished. I was shocked myself. I never knew I had this much good inside of me to take care of this lady.

CHAPTER TWO

Skating By

The bus was filled with students as we got closer to the school, and I knew exactly where everyone sat. The real nerds, not me, were in the first two rows of the bus on the right side as you enter, and the weird kids were directly across from them. The next few rows were the rich, snobby kids. They only rode the bus because they didn't have their driving permit yet since we were all still freshmen or sophomores. The athletes and pretty girls sat in the rows next to the emergency exits, and the popular kids were at the back of the bus. We didn't have our normal spots along with the regular kids, so we sat in the front with the nerds. They reeked of Axe and body odor. Personal hygiene wasn't a virtue for them.

As we were getting off the bus, I noticed the kid that was in our spot didn't get off the bus with us. I wondered what his deal was.

I could predict the day because everything would be the same. As we would get to school, we would hear the overjoyed student who was chosen to welcome the students for the announcements as we came in, *Good morning, Falcons! Welcome back to another day of studies. Let's get going and get after it today!* That same voice would repeat every five minutes until the bell rang for classes at 8:00. That same voice would do the Pledge of Allegiance and morning announcements. I had drama for first period, daily life for second period, U.S History for third, then lunch would start at 11:45. Scoop and I would take an extra 10 minutes at lunch, I would then waltz into Math 102 with Mr. P. Finally, I closed the day with gym. Everything was so predictable it gave me hope that my life could flow as easy as school did although I never had control of my own fate.

There was a new voice on the intercom. It was someone who wasn't as jovial as the normal kid who did the morning announcements.

"Um, good morning everybody welcome to class. Let's have a great class day," the voice said as he stumbled over the announcement.

As Scoop and I walked our classes, I leaned over and asked, "I wonder what happened to the dude who usually does the announcements? Maybe he's sick?"

"Naw. I heard he's never sick. Somebody told me that he never missed a day since he's been enrolled in school. Talk about dedication, right? It couldn't be me," Scoop said, jokingly. "Well look, you down to get to the cafeteria as soon as class is over today? I saw on the South Shore fights Instagram page that two kids are supposed to fight."

"Now you and I both know that these kids here do not know how to fight and have never seen a fight in person. Kids here are too rich and stuck up for that life. The only people that see that type of stuff is me and you. The closest thing they will get to an altercation is cussing and finger pointing." We both laughed hysterically, did our handshake, and went to our separate classes.

After the pledge, the strange voice came on again and said, "Don't forget, today is the last day to submit your permission slips for the Northern Lights trip next month. Only sign your name on the list after you've given your permission slip to the volunteers during your designated lunch time."

I always wanted to go to see the Northern Lights. The only thing was it was cold in Alaska. I knew I lived in Wisconsin, but that was a different cold. I never went on field trips since I've been going to school. I've either never had the money or never wanted to go. But this trip was big because all the sophomores took this trip every year. I've never been out of the city, and the school was paying for it. With all the stuff that had been going on, I could have used a change of scenery for once.

My first two classes flew by like usual. Drama and daily life were easy electives to get A's in. Mrs. Leno's class was a bit more difficult.

"Good morning class! Would you open your books to page 103? I hope you all read the assignment from yesterday. Now what did the Thirteenth Amendment do," Mrs. Leno asked.

She was an old Black teacher who had been teaching for thirty years. One thing I liked about South Shore was that they had Black teachers, White teachers, Hispanic teachers, and Asian teachers. Most ethnic groups were represented and taught at least one class they wanted to teach. Everybody had Mrs. Leno's US History class. She was a fan favorite for most students. I liked her because she didn't teach right out of the book, exclusively. She would engage us in conversation and make us answer questions. At least the other students because I didn't participate. She didn't give out homework either, only tests or quizzes.

"It was an amendment that freed the slaves," one student who raised his hand answered.

"Well, it really didn't free the slaves because there were still some slaves who didn't know that the law had changed, and they were still on the plantation. Some of them couldn't afford to live regular lives because they didn't have the means to support a family from nothing. Even today, if you go to jail or prison, you are technically a slave according to the Thirteenth Amendment."

Mrs. Leno smiled with concern, "Good thinking Isaiah, but the amendment did stop involuntary servitude at that time. Slavery was ended, but if you look closely, it's really not if you're a criminal. Also, there were some people who didn't get the memo that they were free until the confederacy failed in 1865. That's why some Black people celebrate June 19th as Juneteenth because that's when one of the last slaves in Texas finally got word of their freedom two years later."

"So, you're telling me that if I go to jail, technically I'll be a slave?" one student asked. "That is total BS. What is the point of the amendment if I mess up then I have to be a slave?"

"That's what happens when closet racists are pressured on both sides," Isaiah exclaimed.

"Isaiah, is that how we talk in my class?"

"No, Mrs. Leno, but there are so many people who think that this country is for liberty and justice for all, and it's really not. Only liberty and justice for whites. Think about it. I know that you know this, Mrs. Leno, but some of these kids don't know what I'm about to say. After 'freeing the slaves', police were used to capture and round up black people and put them in jail so they could get free labor out of them. Then, years go by after that, Jim Crow came and segregated Black people and whites. And as a side note, Jim Crow was a fake character played by a white man who mocked Black slaves. Up until the civil rights act, segregation was legal. Then to make matters worse, the government killed Black political activists, imported drugs into the inner city that destroyed the Black family, then blamed the Black people about us oppressing ourselves. How can a system created by whites be for freedom for all when they are in control of the system? So, when I say closet racists, I mean people who really don't care about full freedom or liberty especially when their way of life becomes in danger."

This kid just gave an entire dissertation on slavery and segregation at fifteen years old. He sounded like he a sixty-year-old man who studied Black history. I never knew Isaiah personally, but I knew he was very smart because he was a teacher's pet. Teacher's aide was his real title. I never talked to him or anything but after that, hearing the knowledge about Black people made me feel good. It made me feel like somebody actually cared about us. B was white, and I felt like she didn't like me because I was Black. I felt like I was in my own version on the Thirteenth Amendment. I wasn't totally free of B, but I wasn't under the pain of B.

The conversation of the topic kept going and I sunk in my desk and wrote in my notebook until it was time for lunch. As I was walking out of the classroom, Mrs. Leno grabbed my shoulder and instructed me to take a seat and wait for the rest of the students to leave so we could talk.

"I have a bone to pick with you sir." Mrs. Leno scolded. "Why were you so out of it today in class? Normally, you are very quiet, and I get that, but today your posture spoke to me differently."

"Well, there is some stuff going on at home I don't want to talk about, and today hasn't been a great day for me. I think it's because I'm hungry. Can I go to lunch now?"

She tightened her lips and nodded and permitted me to go to lunch. The look on her face right before I left was a look of deep concern. I didn't like talking to people about my business, and I wanted to keep to myself. As I walked through the doorway, Mrs. Leno said, "I want to let you know you're more of a leader than you know it. Oh, and keep writing." I smirked at her and went toward the lunchroom.

As I entered the cafeteria, I heard a commotion and decided to follow the noise. I turned the corner, and I saw two kids arguing and pointing fingers at each other. Curse words filled the space between them as the other students that was circled around them jeered and instigated more animosity. I could tell that they were not used to real fights like I was used to. This would be a typical day in my neighborhood. It got so loud that the liaison broke up the mob before anything could escalate further. Both kids that were arguing got sent to the principal's office. The typical punishment would be in school suspension for the next class and the school would call your parents. I finally went in line for lunch, and Scoop ran behind me excited and, in an uproar, almost knocked over my tray.

"Bro, did you see that? I thought they were about to fight for real! You should have saw it from the beginning it got crazy."

I put my face in my hand and said, "Now you and I both know that there would be no type of fight going on in this type of school. You should know this because we live in the same hood."

After everything calmed down, we started to eat our lunch. As we were nearly finished, I saw the kid who was sitting in our seat on the bus standing near the cafeteria door waiting for the bell to ring.

I nudged Scoop and said, "Hey, that's the kid that was sitting in our spot on the bus. I thought he was going to another school. Maybe his mom was the bus driver." Scoop had a weird look on his face. He started to inch over to him slowly, but before he could walk over there, I grabbed his shoulder.

"Scoop, what are you about to do?" I said nervously.

"I'm about to go introduce myself and ask why he was in our spot on the bus."

"Are you sure that's good idea? We don't know who he is, and he looks like he's just minding his own business right now. Let's just leave him alone, and we can talk to him on the bus when we're going home."

"Nope! I think I'll talk to him now." Scoop walked off toward the kid as I followed behind him. He was a tall, swole guy. He looked like a football player. I hated confrontation and Scoop wanted to walk up to him and say something ignorant to him. I knew he was going to say something that pissed him off.

Scoop walked up to him and said, "I like that chain you go on. Where did you get it from?"

The kid looked at Scoop and said nothing.

"Are you new here?"

The kid said nothing.

"Why aren't you wearing a uniform if you're going here?"

The kid looked at Scoop and looked out the door as he leaned against the wall.

"You ask too many questions, brah," the kid said with an exhausted sound to his voice. Since I knew Scoop's personality, I chimed in quick to calm Scoop down.

"Look bro, he didn't mean to come at you like that. That's our bad. His name is Gary, but everybody calls him Scoop and my name is James, but you can call me J. We really don't see anybody that looks like us in this school too often. You can look around and see who goes here. We'll let you go to class, bro."

The kid looked at me slightly relieved and said, "It's all good, man. It's been a crazy few days for me, but I'll get through it. I'm Malcom." He put his hand out, so we all shook hands.

"Since we all just became homies, I just want to let you know that you were in our spot this morning on the bus. We had to sit by the lame niggas," Scoop said with a smirk on his face.

"I heard what you was saying on the bus. I was about to get up and say something to you, but today was my first day and I didn't want to get in trouble." Scoop laughed nervously, "Anyways, what is that Northern Light trip?"

Scoop replied, "It's in Alaska and every year all the tenth graders go. This school got so many rich white folks donating that everyone that signs up can go for free. You should come with us to sign up. We only got a few minutes."

"Yeah, it's cool with me," Malcom said, "I don't have anything going on since football season is over."

I forgot I needed to have my permission slip signed. B had been out of it since her fall, so I had to figure out a way to get it signed.

"Scoop, I don't have my permission slip signed."

"Bro, are you stupid?"

"B's been hurt, bro. She can't move or do anything for herself right now."

"All right, I'll go make a copy of mine in the library and white it out so you can sign her name."

"Nigga, that will not work," I said with fear in my heart.

"Yes, it will. Hold up, let me run there really quick."

Scoop ran as fast as he could to the library and made it back to the cafeteria in three minutes flat. He was out of breath, but he did a good job making it look like an empty permission slip where his dad had signed. I grabbed a pen out of my backpack and signed Beatrice Lewis on the parent or guardian section. I held it up and looked at it to make sure it looked right. I shrugged with a shaky acceptance.

"Here Malcom, I made two copies. Just sign your mom or dad's name so you can go."

"Dad."

He looked at Scoop firmly.

"Ok," Scoop said confused, "Let's turn these in and bounce." We all shook hands again and went to our separate classes.

When I was walking to my next class, Mrs. Leno's words began to replay in my mind, "You're more of a leader than you know it." I knew what she meant but I didn't know how to accept it. How could I be a leader in the situation that I was facing? If controlling your emotions were apart of leadership then I failed that test two months ago when I yelled at B. I've always wanted to be in control of the situations I got myself into. I guess that could be a part of leadership.

February 17ᵗʰ Skate: Mrs. Leno's Class

Walk tall and jump to the heights you decide. Skip the steps of the dope sell and sell dope dreams to the lives that can't afford to fail. Life is translucent not a reflection. So fragile right? Too much? Wait! Think before you speak, you're on thin ice. Tread lightly. Better yet skate with elegance. The ones before you push you and the ones after you lean on you so don't melt, YOU JUST MATTER. Not transparent but a likeness to who you are made to be. So, when life seems too far down to see, keep on skating because your eyes are meant more than just to physically see.

The final bell rang for school to let out. Scoop and I met at our usual spot outside for the bus. We looked behind us and we saw Malcom walking toward us with someone else beside him. Scoop tapped my shoulder and asked, "Who is that with your boy Malcom?"

I squinted to focus on who the person was. As they came closer, I leaned over to him and said, "Oh that's Isaiah from my U.S History class. You know this kid gave a whole Martin Luther King speech about slavery?"

"You know how them rich niggas be acting," Scoop snarled.

As they approached us, Malcom shook our hand and introduced Isaiah to us. "This is my homie, Isaiah. I met him in my physics class today. He said he's going on the Northern Lights trip too. We should see if we can all room together since we are the only Black dudes in the tenth grade."

Scoop and I looked at each other and shrugged our shoulders in agreement.

Isaiah chuckled and said, "You don't know how long I have been waiting to be friends with the other Black people in this school. Don't get me wrong, I have friends, other Black friends, but not at the school. I already know who you are James."

I was confused on how he knew my name. I never introduced myself to him or even talked to him because I never said my name in class.

"Wait, how do you know my name?" I asked.

"You know we have U.S History together, right? I see you in the back writing and pretending not to pay attention all the time. And secretly I compete with you in that class."

"Why would you compete with me?"

"I stay after school to help Mrs. Leno once in a while, and I see your work and how you think. Your writing skill are amazing. You're in the top of the class and it seems like you have no interest. You have so much potential to be the best, but it seems as if you're always distant when you're there."

"Well, that's kind of who I am. I'm not outgoing or anything. I'm chill. That's just me"

"To be honest, I think you and I can be at the top of the class when we graduate. That is how much potential I think you have. You should think about the early graduation program."

"I'll think about it."

I'd never had anyone my age speak to me like that. Sure, I had a few teachers tell me something similar, but their job is to get the most out of their students. What did Isaiah and Mrs. Leno see in me that I didn't see in myself? I didn't know how to react to those words. I was going to simply laugh it off.

Scoop chimed in, "Now that the Motivation Monday is over, we got a bus to get on."

"My uncle coming to pick me and Malcom up since he lives by me, did you want him to give you two a ride home too? I can text him?" Isaiah suggested.

I figured the day was already a funky one, so we decided to catch a ride. We all talked and laughed for a while. Before we knew it, Isaiah's uncle came and blew the horn for us to get in his truck. As we got in, there was a girl that caught the corner of my eye. I couldn't get a real good look at her appearance. I had to hurry up and find her before we pulled off. Dating wasn't something high on my priority list at the time, but the glimpse of her resonated with me. I couldn't wait to get to school the next day to find her.

"This is my Uncle Tee, he's in the Army and is getting deployed over in Iraq tomorrow."

Isaiah's uncle was a tall and muscular man that looked like he was built for combat. He was the epitome of a solider and had that look. "How many people have you shot since you've been in the army, Unc?" Isaiah asked.

"I haven't shot anyone just yet. We don't even know if we are even going to fight anybody. But once we get there I'll write and keep you updated. By the way, are we all going to the same place or what? I have to go visit some people, but I'll stop by your dad for a little while."

Isaiah insisted we all go to his house. When we entered his neighborhood, it looked exactly like the neighborhood I saw in my visions. There were kids playing outside, the lawns were perfectly cut, and everyone looked friendly. Who knew that the place where Isaiah lived was less than two miles away from where I lived?

As we got out of the car, I nudged Scoop and said, "I don't know why your mom and dad choose to live in the hood. They can afford to live over here with these people."

"My dad said the best way to see real change is from the inside out. He stayed instead of leaving so there's a little help here. He got a few houses around the block so the hood don't look as bad. I like our neighborhood. It feels like home to me. Besides, we ain't that rich, bro. We got a little change, but our pockets ain't this deep. I wonder how Isaiah's parents got out here with the white people?"

I gazed at the front of Isaiah's house.

"Yeah, I hear what you're saying. I wouldn't mind living in a house like this."

I looked up and the birds were different. They had nests for their offspring in the trees. The air was clear, and the atmosphere was pleasant. There weren't helicopters and sirens blazing. You could hear nature being one with its residents.

As we walked through the front door, the aroma of food cooking filled the air. I heard pots and pans clanging together and vegetables being chopped on a cutting board. A pile of shoes lay to the side. We all took our shoes off and we followed Isaiah to the kitchen. I was amazed when I saw stainless steel appliances and an island in the middle of the kitchen. Isaiah's mom was cooking.

"Good afternoon boys. I didn't know Isaiah was bringing over company, or I would have made more food."

"No need, they're not staying. Uncle T is dropping everybody off. He wanted to stop by before he left today."

"Oh well that's too bad." Isaiah's mom replied. "Well, all of you are welcome to stay if you like. Just call your parents before you do, ok?"

We all said thank you in sync with each other. Isaiah showed us to the living room, and I felt the soft carpet running across my heel because there was a hole in my sock. The living room was bright and lit up. I caught the smell of fresh air from the large window that was open.

He had a 55-inch flat screen TV mounted above the fireplace. I went and sat on the leather couch and stared at the paintings and sculptures. It looked as if they'd gotten them from an African Safari. As I looked up, you could see the upstairs portion of the house where the rooms were. I wondered if he had ever tried to jump from the ledge and land on the couch? Wonder filled my mind of living in this type of home. I would have never imagined a kid who looks like me living in this type of place of this city.

"How is it going fellas?" Isaiah's dad came downstairs and greeted everyone. He was a tall burley man with a thick beard. His voice carried significance when he spoke. It was like he commanded attention when he walked in.

"Isaiah, I see you made some new friends."

"Hey, dad, this is Malcom, he's new to the school, and I said he could come over because he lives close by, this is James, we have U.S History class together, and this is...I didn't get his name." Before Scoop could even say anything stupid, I chimed in.

"This is my friend Gary, nice to meet you, sir."

He came around to all of us and shook all our hands like we were businessmen. I noticed that he wore a necklace with a cross on it. I thought he must have been a preacher of some sort.

"Excuse me, I like the chain you have on, where did you get it from?" Scoop had a thing with chains. Scoop was never afraid to ask anything to anybody. That was one of the things his dad taught him.

Isaiah's dad replied,

"I didn't buy it, but I received it when I was first ordained a minister. Do you and your parents attend the church?" Malcom and I shook our heads no, but Scoop answered.

"Yes, we go to church at Glorious Name Church."

"Oh yes, I know Pastor Glenn well. We went to high school together and worked for the same company before I became a pastor full time. He was the first person I ordained when I became Bishop. He is a very good preacher and good man. Make sure you all stay there because he is anointed. Mr. Malcom would your parents like to attend our church?" Malcom stood with arrogance next to the couch exactly how he stood when we saw him in the lunchroom.

"Naw, church really isn't our style," he said with a smirk. "My dad told me the truth about God and that guy isn't real. It sounds like a fairy tale to me." I looked at Isaiah's face and he looked excited. I was puzzled because this kid just insulted his religion and was excited.

"Bishop Carter, can I handle this one?" Isaiah asked his dad. He nodded and gave him the ok.

"Let me ask you this, Malcom. If you are in an empty room by yourself, and you walk out of the room and five minutes later come back in, and there is a glass of water in the middle of the floor, what would you say?"

Malcom replied, "Who else came in the room?"

"Exactly, there had to be someone who put that glass of water there. Same thing with the earth. Scientists all agree that the earth had a beginning and since the earth came to existence, the only logical explanation is that there was a cause of the earth."

I was never a religious person, but what Isaiah explained flew right over my head. I thought they only used the bible to argue points of God, well at least that's what they normally do. Malcom began to ask follow-up questions, and Isaiah and his dad gave him lengthy answers. That went on for about five minutes, then Isaiah's uncle started getting impatient.

"Can we wrap this bible study up because I have to get going soon. So, who's going where?"

"Scoop and I can walk from here. We don't live too far from here." I wanted to walk to get a better look at the neighborhood. I didn't know when the next time I would be on the good side of town.

"I can walk with them; I live only a few houses down from here," Malcom replied.

"Oh, ok, great. Hopefully I will see you guys in about fourteen months. Nephew, big brother," he yelled in the direction of the kitchen, "sister in-law, I will try and make it back tonight, so I can see you all before I leave in the morning. If not, I love you all, and I will let you know when I make it safely."

They hugged each other and he left through the front door. So far it seemed as if Isaiah was living the life I wanted for myself. He was lucky to have his family that cooked fresh meals, supplied him with a beautiful home, love, and everything a teenager could want he had. I would kill to have had his life. Scoop, Malcom, and I walked toward the front door and picked out our shoes, preparing to leave.

"One day you all should visit the church on a Sunday. I promise you it will be something you have never experienced before," his dad said.

"If it's anything like this house, then I will definitely be there," Scoop replied. Bishop Carter laughed while Isaiah walked with us outside.

"We really should kick it before going on the Northern Lights trip," Isaiah remarked.

"Yeah, that will be pretty dope. I'll see y'all tomorrow at school."

I was always reluctant to make new friends. My only other friend was Scoop. I figured I'd just go with the flow. Malcom walked the opposite way, and Scoop and I talked about how huge Isaiah's house was the whole walk home. I passed Isaiah's neighborhood plenty of times on the bus, but to see this part of town with a different viewpoint was a new experience. You could smell and hear the difference in the air. Your skin felt different. It seemed brighter on the other side of town. I hoped that I would make that thirty-minute walk back home more often now that I knew Isaiah. As we reached the bus stop by my house, I felt the dark cloud coming back over me. An eerie feeling of hopelessness jumped on me.

Back to reality.

I walked in the house and went straight to the basement and plopped on the bed with my clothes still on. My face planted in my pillow, I began crying. Everything that I wanted to be and everything that I was all became unbearable. I was at the point where I wanted everything to end. I didn't care about friends, school, and especially B. I thought no one would miss me if I were gone so why not end it all. I sat up at the edge of the bed with my hand rubbing my face up and down like I wanted to pull it off. Going to Isaiah's house that day triggered me to face something I'd never thought I would face.

Death.

At fifteen, I knew I should not have these thoughts, but when life came crashing down out of nowhere, what other option did I have? That cloud that was over me began to create a storm I couldn't outrun. I thought that it would be with me forever. The best way for me to get rid of the cloud was to go silently.

How could I do that? I was already in enough pain, so I should do it without having to feel anything. I went to the bathroom and looked in the medicine cabinet where B kept her medicine. There were ten orange bottles that I could choose from, so I got two from each bottle. As the pills flipped through my hand, my tears created a small puddle on the floor. I closed the medicine cabinet and on the other side was a mirror. My eyes were bloodshot red and puffy, my cheeks were streaked with tears as I stared at my reflection. I thought to myself, this is it, the pain will be over soon. Taking my own life would be the only time I had control of anything. My whole life, I never had the chance to do what I wanted to do. I always looked out for other people ahead of myself. But with death in the palm of my hand, I felt I had real power.

My hand was shaking as I turned on the sink water, I stuffed the pills in my mouth and heard a voice say my name,

"James."

I turned around and looked to see who else was in the bathroom, and I was alone. Then I heard my name again a little louder,

"James."

I spit all the pills into my hand and stuck them in my pocket and walked into the hallway. It was B. She was in her wheelchair, sitting in the middle of the hallway. I walked up to her with disbelief. The doctor said she would have trouble speaking for a while, but it has only been about two months. She gained strength in her arms to roll herself from the living room into the hallway.

She struggled to open her mouth to speak but eventually said,

"Your life is not over. We need you." She then bowed her head down and went to sleep.

In total shock, I woke up in a cold sweat fully dressed in the basement. I never left my bed from when I came in the house that evening. I rolled over and looked at the time on my phone. It was 11:59 PM, then the clock struck midnight. The fact that B spoke and said that "we need you" had to be a dream because that woman would never say anything like that. I went upstairs to the bathroom to make sure what I experienced was a dream.

I turned the water on and cupped my hands and massaged the water in my face. As drips of water pelted in the sink, I reached over to the hand towel and dried my face. I stared at myself in the mirror, and it seemed as if my life flashed before my eyes.

I saw my father being dragged away from me in cuffs. I saw B's anger and rage at me the past five years. Everything that made my life miserable attacked my mind. I decided to open the cabinet. I lifted my hand to open it but what kept playing in my head was "your life is not over, we need you." I reluctantly closed the cabinet and went to check on B. Even though it was a dream, I felt as if I didn't hear those words in a dream. As I walked through the hallway and into the living room, I saw B in her wheelchair asleep with the TV on with her fists clinched. I had forgot to feed her after I came home from Isaiah's. I rustled up some soft food to feed to her and wrote before I went to sleep.

Beauty February 18th

Sleep evades. It seems like a façade. Striking 12, the day is over, it's all odd. Insomnia and repression, displaced aggression. Seems like life's a cruel lesson. Don't listen to the clouds, or else rain is your depression. Out of focus but you catch a glimpse of beauty. Beautiful shades of black. In the arms of the shadows, right at home, and relaxed.

CHAPTER THREE

No New Friends

The next day I slept past my alarm, so I was running late. I jumped out of bed and hurried to get my bearings about myself; however, I could not stop thinking about the dream I'd had the night before. I didn't want to miss the bus, so I needed to put that thought behind me. I did my morning routine: Clean B, change B, feed B, and put B back in front of the TV and put on her shows. After that, I would get myself ready for school. As I walked past B to get to the door, her blanket had fallen. I bent down and put it back on her. When I spread it across her lap, she reached up to me as if she wanted a hug. I obliged and leaned in and hugged her.

It was more awkward than the dream I had the night before. As I walked out the door, I had a crazy thought. *Maybe she changed.* The doctor did say that she could have an altered personality, but I wouldn't hold my breath on that.

I proceeded to the bus stop and saw Scoop standing waiting on me. I laughed a little because that was the first time he had ever beaten me there. He was looking at his wrist as if he was clocking the time. I walked up to him as I laughed and greeted him with our handshake.

"Man, what are you doing here so early? Your mom and dad must have kicked you out the house for you to beat me here."

Scoop had a big grin on his face and replied,

"Nope you're wrong. I got some good news, and I wanted you to be the first to know. You know that senior chick Tiffany? She's digging your boy. She liked five of my pictures on Instagram last night. I'm telling you I'm about to bag her. See I told you I got that juice."

Tiffany was the most popular girl in school because she was social media famous. She had over 1,000,000 followers on TikTok and Instagram combined and 800,000 subscribers on YouTube. She walked around the school recording herself and her friends all day. She did makeup tutorials and did vegan recipe reviews. In other words, she was out of Scoop's league.

With an exaggerated shocked look on my face I said,

"Stop playing. Let me see which one's she liked."

I scrolled through his phone and the only pictures she liked was inspirational quotes he posted.

"Hate to break it to you but she don't like you, bro. Hang it up because she didn't even like the pictures you were even in. You got so many hashtags in the captions that plenty of people liked it. To make matters worse, she didn't even like five pictures in a row. They were all scattered. So better luck next time."

With his face scrunched Scoop exclaimed,

"For the record, I want you to know that you're a hater."

The bus approached us, and Scoop pulled out his bus pass for the first time in forever. Only a girl could make Scoop wake up early and remember his bus pass. Even though I could always count on Scoop to change the temperature of my day, the climate of my life was always unrelenting. I didn't know how to process what happened between B and me. The only way I could manage my emotions would be to put on the mask I've learned to wear every day.

I noticed neither Shane nor the woman bus driver from the day before was driving the bus. It was an older man driving. We showed him our bus passes and went to our spots and chatted all the way to school.

I looked out of the window and saw Malcom and Isaiah standing in front of the bus stop at school as if they were waiting on us. Scoop and I decided to meet them there. We came near them and Isaiah waved at us with a smile. I felt hesitant to befriend Isaiah and Malcom. Since I was going with the flow, I made the decision not to open up to them as much but in the same breath, keep myself from making enemies.

"Malcom, did you know the lady that was driving the bus yesterday? Because we thought she was related to you since you were on the bus before us?" Scoop questioned.

"I don't know who that lady was. But she knew stuff about me that only my dad would know. That was kind of wild to be honest."

Scoop replied, "All the bus drivers that pick-up students on academy busses are told information about the students that go to South Shore. Since almost every kid that goes here has money, the school wants staff to know whose kid they are dealing with if there is ever an incident. It's part of the 'South Shore' way. You'll learn that if you're here long enough because they brainwash it into all their students. I think it's weird. This is a school that made sure that the students knew they were in a privileged position. Before they accept you to attend the school, they did a background check on the students and their parents. They would collect the parents' employment information so they could make sure they can afford the tuition of the school."

The 'South Shore' way was something Scoop made up because he felt like the school shouldn't have to know all that information in order for kids to attend. His dad was upset about that, and Scoop almost went to Tech on the North side of the city our freshman year. The reason he didn't go is because Scoop's dad was going to send him to an HBCU after high school so he would be around Black people the rest of his life.

Every time Scoop's dad would talk to us about life he would always say, *"Make sure when you go to this school, you give everything you got and learn the ways of each person in there. No matter if they are Black, White, Latino, or Asian. Once you learn how to maneuver with different people, that's when you can pull their resources and bring it back to your community."* He was all about community and helping the fellow Black man. But he never mistreated or spoke badly about any other race. He respected everyone but revered the Black community.

"All right guys, since we all have the same lunch, we should all sit by each other and start preparing for this trip next month," Isaiah chimed in.

I didn't want to sit by them because Scoop and I would usually sit in our own spot. I needed to make up a lie real fast so I could get out of it.

"I have to stay after US History and talk about our last assignment."

"You got an A, what do you have to talk about? Isaiah said. "We can talk about it after school because I'm going to Malcom's house to help him with the test we have coming up. He has Mrs. Leno's class first period. So, you can meet us in the cafeteria. Maybe you can come over with us if it is all right with Malcom's dad?"

"Trust me, it'll be ok for him to come over. Dad's in Jacksonville holding private workouts this weekend. He won't be back until Monday or Tuesday," Malcom replied.

"What does your dad do?" Scoop asked. "Is he some sort of body builder or YouTube personal trainer? They make bank, so I see how you can afford to come here. At first, I thought you were here on a football scholarship or something."

Malcom chuckled with arrogance, "Well technically, I did earn a football scholarship; my dad did play a little football professionally. Now he trains upcoming college players on their way to get drafted in the first round."

"Now I know who you are," Scoop blurted out, "Your dad is Jermaine Taylor that played running back! That dude was crazy good. Why did he retire so early? He should definitely be in the Hall of Fame. Nobody did what he did in a short period of time. He could still play right? Yeah, J let's go to his house after school today!"

Scoop was a little too excited to hear that Malcom's dad played in the NFL. It was cool hearing that, and I could tell that Malcom liked telling people about his dad. When Scoop started going off, Malcom's body language changed to cocky from relaxed. Praise was his safe place. We talked about his dad and what it was like being a son of a celebrity for a while. I soaked everything in because I envied Malcom's life. I had a bad habit of wanting other people's lives. I'd give anything to get out of my situation.

Isaiah and Malcom had similar lives, except it seemed like Malcom's dad was never home, so he had to fend for himself on most days. I figured it wouldn't be a bad idea to go to Malcom's house because I wanted to live vicariously through him this time. Plus, I knew Scoop would want to go, and if he went without me, I knew he would do something really stupid, so I accepted the invitation. I just hoped I wouldn't dream again about killing myself afterwards.

"We're about to be late. Let's just meet at lunch so Scoop can finish drooling over your dad." Isaiah said.

Everybody laughed and we all went to our classes.

When we met in the cafeteria, we laughed and talked as if we'd been friends for years. I usually only felt this comfortable around Scoop. It was something about these other two that clicked with us. Scoop was more like Malcom and I was more like Isaiah. Malcom had a cool arrogance about him. He was brash and talk-ative. Isaiah was more reserved and calculated in his conversation. The difference between him and me was he gave off an aura of success and discipline. Opening to new people was hard for me, but there was something about Isaiah that made me want to talk and express myself.

Most of the time, change was bad for me because that meant my routine would be different. I was always predictable in what I did, but with this new change of scenery and new friends, I was in a bit of a predicament. At this point, the only thing I could do was not fight it but go with the flow.

School was dismissed and we met at the same bus stop as that morning. Malcom suggested that we get a ride from him today since he got his car out of the shop. We walked to the student parking lot, and he had a black 2017 Hellcat. To say that his car was beautiful would be an understatement. I had never seen a car of this kind before in person let alone ride in one.

"Hey Malcom, how close do you live to Isaiah?" I asked.

"I live just a few houses down from him."

Isaiah hopped in the front seat while Scoop and I went into the back. Malcom jumped in the driver seat, started the car, and violently revved the engine. It was loud. Loud enough to drown out Scoop screaming next to me in the back seat.

Once the revving stopped Scoop leaned over to me and whispered, "We need to keep them around, bro. They might just rub off on us."

I smiled and looked out the window only to see the girl that caught my eye the day before. She was a brown beauty. This time she saw me in the car and looked at me. My heart sunk in nervousness. I felt on the inside that I wanted to talk to her, but my brain was telling me not to. Sometimes I hated being me because of my timidity. That made me think about what Scoop just said.

Maybe some of what Malcom and Isaiah had would rub off on me. Confidence and boldness.

We arrived at Malcom's house and it was at least twice the size of Isaiah's. In the driveway was a Mercedes, BMW, Tesla, two Lamborghinis, and a Bentley. It felt as if I was looking at a rainbow with how many colors they had. We walked in the house and Malcom showed us around.

"All right guys, let me give you the grand tour. If you look up, we got a nice chandelier that costs $50,000. If we go to our left, we have sitting room number one. This is where my dad has meetings with local people like plumbers and electricians when there is an issue. Follow me down the hall and you will see the living room with our 88-inch Ultra 4k TV. This is where I play 2k and Call of Duty on PS5. Walk with me here to our kitchen where we have a personal chef prep all our meals. Of course, we have high grade granite counter tops. On the left, is the guest room and the den is on the right. Now, we will enter my dad's office, or what I like to call the glory room."

The room was riddled with trophies, articles, medals, and pictures with other celebrities. MVP trophies, college football championship rings, pictures with Barak and Michelle Obama.

Malcom took a deep breath and said,

"My dad is crazy accomplished at what he did. Coming from the hood it was wild he even went to college. I don't want to be just like him. I want to be better than him. Whenever I get pissed off after practice or a bad game, I come in here to look at greatness and get my powers back up."

With gazing eyes Scoop says,

"What is your room looking like, though?"

Scoop has never held his tongue. Even though his parents did well, this was something he had never seen in person. I could tell by the look in his eyes that he was just as elated as me to be in the house of a millionaire. He was taking it all in and left nothing unsaid.

"I bet being in this big house gets lonely sometimes, doesn't it? With you dad always on the road you're by yourself. Where is your mom? Does she travel with your dad?" Scoop asked as we walked up the spiral staircase.

Malcom, who was walking in front of us, stopped right before he turned the handle of his room door and looked down the hall then said, "You remember the other day when I said you ask too many questions? You are asking too many questions. Some things I don't talk about and that's one of them."

After he finished speaking, I could see a hurt in his eyes. He opened the door to his room, and it was filled with every high school kid dream. Flat screen TV and an Xbox with all the games, a basketball rim connected to his wall, a king-sized bed, and a closet full of clothes and every pair of shoes you can imagine. He even had a mini-fridge filled with sodas and snacks. I glared in amazement at the room and immediately imagined that it was my room. I would come in and kick off my shoes by the doorway and grab a soda before I decided which game system I would play. After that, I would lie down on the king-size bed and look up and watch the ceiling fan until I went to sleep.

"Yo, this room is dope. When can we spend the night?" Scoop asked.

"You are kind of pushy, huh? I'm sure when he wants us to spend the night, he will let us. It is no big deal to me," Isaiah answered.

"Yeah, that's because you got a mini-mansion like his, so it wouldn't be a big deal for you. I bet your dad got all that money from the people giving in that big church. Skimming some off the top right? I know all about churches like that."

"Wait, didn't you tell my dad you went to another church the other day? Why do you go if you think they are stealing money?"

"I only go because my mom and dad make me. I know the game all too well, man. You can't fool me."

"Let me ask you this then; do you think it's ok for the pastor of the church to get paid?" Isaiah asked.

"No. First, they ask for hundreds of dollars nine or ten times when it's time to give money. Then they auction people down from $100 to $50 all the way down to pennies. That is stealing money from the people. Second, these pastors are grown men with families, they shouldn't have to rely on the hard-earned money of the people that go there. Some people have bills and kids to take care of, but they are busy being sold a dream that they are going to be millionaires if they give their rent money. It's all a scam if you ask me."

"Well, Scoop, I could articulate the system which God has put in place more elegantly than that soliloquy you provided us with. I could tell you about how God placed the system of giving and receiving and sowing and reaping in the beginning of the world which was hijacked for what most people call 'Karma.' I could tell you about how the bible speaks about how pastors should be paid for the work they do leading a church. I could also tell you about all the business ventures my dad had before he started pastoring. And, I bet some of the movies you have watched were written by my dad. So, before you rant about how pastors are thieves and bad people, especially my father, I would appreciate it if you would do some research beforehand. I mean that in the most respectful way possible."

Malcom and I stood dumbfounded at how passive aggressive Isaiah was. Then we burst out laughing on the floor. We were holding our stomachs in pain at how funny that was. Scoop stood there making faces, mocking us because he was embarrassed at what was said.

Finally, after we started quieting down from laughing Isaiah interjected and said, "Look, man, I didn't mean it for them to think it was funny, but I just get very upset about how people view pastors and money in the church, especially my dad. You don't know how many times I have to defend this subject on IG and Twitter."

"Yeah, whatever, bro. Anyways, J what time are we leaving? I gotta get home soon," Scoop said sharply.

"I can give you guys a ride home if you like. We just have to stop by my house to pick up my car," Isaiah offered.

"Naw, we good, bro," Scoop replied irritably. "Malcom, thanks for inviting us over, bro. We can walk to our house from here."

I've seen Scoop angry to the point of him arguing then fighting. He wasn't angry at this point; he was too embarrassed to come back at Isaiah. I thought I would have never saw the day someone would shut Scoop up in the most respectful way possible. I was timidly gratified about it, but I made sure to keep that emotion to myself because he was already humiliated. We went downstairs, put our shoes on, and left the house. As soon as we turned the corner and passed Isaiah's house Scoop broke the silence.

"I'm going to tell you this now, bro. I don't like that Isaiah dude."

"What happened? We were hanging out all day long, laughing and joking until the thing about church came up. It's not even him who brought it up. It was you."

"Look, I don't care who brought what up, he didn't have to come at me like that. What made it worse was you was over there chuckling your guts out with Malcom. It wasn't funny at all."

"Scoop, just listen to yourself, man. You upset about some church kid having more information about how that Bible stuff works. He's been in church his whole life and you and your parents just started going not too long ago. I think you just need to relax."

I've always tried to calm Scoop down when it came to confrontations. He was the instigator and I was the mediator. Ever since I've known Scoop, he's been that way. At this point of my life, making his problems mine was not high on my priority list. I was his protector and his get out of jail free card. I didn't know how much more I could take at this point. My routine being broken and the stress of B started taking its toll.

"As long as I've known you who has always taken your side? Me. I'm the one who has gotten you out of fights, arguments, and everything. To be completely honest, being your friend is exhausting."

I felt the same rush of emotions come over me as it did with B when she fell. I knew what I was saying, but I could not control it. This time it was with my best and only friend. I wanted to shut up, but my mouth wouldn't let the words stay hidden. I was in a tug of war with my thoughts and my heart. My heart said talk it out and don't make things worse, but my thoughts said tell him what you think. My thoughts won and by the time I wanted to change what I did, it was too late.

"Where is this coming from? We supposed to be boys. I don't know them like that, so why would I take their side? Isaiah gave you a taste of your own medicine and you can't handle it. Stop being soft."

"You know what," Scoop said with disappointment, "I really don't have to take this from a foster kid. I should have known all along that you never knew what loyalty was. You meet two new people and all of a sudden you start acting brand new. Don't even trip."

Typical Scoop. We would have arguments like this periodically, so I thought nothing of it. I usually gave him a day or two to cool down, and he would ask for me to come over, and we would be cool again.

Toxic.

We had plans to be successful together until our old age. We thought we would be those old guys who went to their favorite restaurant at 6:30 in the morning and talk about the good old days and politics. All relationships have issues.

After the overwhelming emotions, Scoop took the opposite way under the train tracks to his house and I took the regular route through the neighborhood. As I progressed from the wealthy neighborhood to the middle-class neighborhood, to where we lived, that's when everything went gray again. I felt in myself a shift take place. Oddly, at this point, I was almost relieved to get home to take care of B.

February 19th

I don't feel like being creative today. I won't bore you with fire bars or haiku's today. I need to get something out. My only friend left me, and I feel ok about it. It's weird to say that, but maybe this was the shakeup I needed. One day I'll look back at this note-book and laugh about how dumb this argument was. Don't get me wrong, Scoop was, or should I say is my guy, but he gets into his feelings easily. He wears his emotions on his sleeve and that's ok, he will come back around. He always does. What's crazy is, ever since Malcom came on the bus two days ago, my routine has been all jacked up. Now that I think about it, Malcom may be a bad energy or something. But that girl noticed me today in the car. Maybe his energy isn't that bad. I don't know why I have never seen her at school before today. The year is almost over, and in the year and a half at South Shore this chick has never crossed my path. Well, I guess we will see how this plays out. I'll let Scoop come back to his senses, and I will try to get something to say to this girl. Hopefully she doesn't have a boyfriend.

February 23rd Ledge

Be this. Be that. Do this. What is the point? Can you really see the street from here? Don't jump because the fall will kill you.

Jump because we can save you. Who's telling the truth? See from here the water looks shallow. Objects from the top look smaller than they may appear. From here I have a better view than you. I see further and longer. Nothing obstructing my sight. What's big to you is small to me, so I guess I'll stay up here a little longer.

New Beginnings

Everything was different since Scoop and I had the argument that rocked our friendship. A week went by, and I hadn't heard a word from him. It was different because, usually, we would make up a day after an argument. I went to the bus alone, I ate lunch alone, I walked the halls alone, and I went back home alone. I saw Scoop around the halls but nowhere else. I saw him getting a ride from his mom to and from school.

Silence became normal after only a week. What became wildly normal was being B's caretaker. Even though I had to wait on her hand and foot, she was becoming less of a burden on me. In return, she had become nicer by hugging me every day. I thought that some of the dream actually manifested. What shocked me was that the house started to feel like home. I would come home to B smiling at me and trying to talk to me instead of her yelling. Her eyes looked more calming instead of her normal yellow-ish glare deep in my soul. I was feeding her healthy foods like fruits and vegetables. She started losing weight and her skin appeared clearer. My rollercoaster of a life had always been full of ups and downs. This time it was on the upward swing.

My alarm sounded and I began my day. There was a thunderstorm outside, and I didn't have an umbrella. I stood outside while waiting for the bus, and my hood had gotten soaking wet, and the water started seeping through the cotton, making my hair damp. Tiny drops of water slid down my nose onto the concrete. I leaned forward to prevent a puddle from forming on the top of my head. I cupped my hands together to catch the raindrops. Slowly, the rain from my hood swam its way through the cracks of my fingers while the rain from the sky splashed its way into a new puddle. The process started over again. New rain turned into a puddle in my hand and slowly vanished through my fingers. I looked at the drops of water that landed in my hand. Each raindrop was distinct, even though it came from the same cloud. The same type of water could cause a flood, destroy things, and even drown people. Or they could help plants grow, refill rivers, and cleanse. Clouds weren't so bad after all. Today, I felt clean.

I saw Isaiah pull up to the corner at the bus stop in his car. As I approached him, he rolled down the window and yelled out, "It's raining so hop in!" I got into his car, and he pulled off to school.

"How did you know where my bus stopped at?" I inquired.

"Malcom told me where your stop was yesterday. Where is Scoop and why haven't you been talking to us? It's been a week and you looked right passed me every day last week. Even at lunch, you and Scoop don't even sit by each other. That's why I came by and picked you up because I wasn't sure if I did something to make you mad, but Scoop, I understand why he isn't talking to us."

At this point I was unsure if I should tell him or not. Yes, we had a little bond, but I haven't known him for any good length of time. Yet, there was something about him that made me want to pour my heart out. I decided to tell him why I avoided them.

"Well, my personality is not like everybody's. When you and Scoop had that little dispute, I didn't want to make matters worse by talking with you and Malcom. Lately my mouth has been getting me into trouble, and I normally don't do that."

While trying to keep his eyes on the road, Isaiah slightly leaned over and replied, "I understand your loyalty. I understand what it means to be loyal to your convictions to a fault. I'm going to be straight up and ask you, what is your story?"

I knew exactly what he meant by that question. I wanted to avoid it, but something kept pulling me in to answer the question. I decided to play dumb.

"I don't know what you mean by my story?"

"What I mean is, what does your parents do? Why are you the way you are? That's what I mean. If you don't want to talk about it, then it is totally cool with me. I hate it when people want me to talk about stuff when I don't want to. My dad does it all the time."

I thought that I would use his dad as a deflection to not talk about me. I felt relieved. I took a deep breath and decided to ask him the same question he asked me.

"Well, what's your story? How does it feel to be Mr. Perfect?"

Isaiah leaned forward and looked both ways before he proceeded to cross the four-way stop. There was a thirty-second pause of silence as he slowed the car down and stopped a block before the school.

He took a deep breath and said, "Listen, I know that everybody has that perception of me. Everybody thinks that I have my life figured out, and I have everything right going for me. Albeit that may be true, I'm still a teenager like everyone else. I know I don't sound like a normal teenager, but I still have the same struggles that you have. Most people don't understand the struggle that I go through. I have a mom who is a New York Times best-selling author, a twin sister who has straight A's and is set up to go to Howard on a full scholarship, and a dad who made millions as a writer before he developed the church into a mega church. Before all the money and the fame, my mom and dad were dead broke. Welfare, food stamps, the whole nine. I wasn't born during the grunt of their struggle, but my uncle remembers those days like it was yesterday. One day I'll ask my dad to tell you the full story, but with all this pressure I have on me to succeed, it is hard to feel normal at times. The only thing that keeps me grounded is my faith in God. I know two things: the first thing is that he will never leave me or forsake me, and the second thing is I know that someone always has it worse than I do. I know I'm in a privileged position for a Black kid, and I want to share what I have with people like you. I know you're in a tough spot, but I know God will guide you through your life. Even in your house, God sees your heart and how you are caring for someone that doesn't deserve it. He will reward you for that."

At that moment, I lost my breath as I sank into the leather of the seat. I thought to myself, how could he know about B? How could he know that I am taking care of her? How could he know she treated me badly? It dawned on me that Scoop may have told him something before they fell out. I was able to gather myself and not fall into the mysticism. I pushed myself from inside of the seat and straightened up and let him finish talking.

Once there was an opening for me to speak, I said "I didn't mean to piss you off calling you Mr. Perfect. I didn't know that about your family. Thank you for being concerned about me, but how did you know about my situation? With me taking care of someone who doesn't deserve it. Because I'm kind of in a situation now like that, but I don't want to go too much into detail. Did Scoop tell you anything?"

Isaiah lightly giggled, "No, Scoop didn't tell me anything. There is this thing that happens to me when I start talking to people about certain things, I get information in my head them."

"Like a psychic?"

"Um, I wouldn't call it that, but that isn't important."

"Either way it goes, that was weird," I remarked, "We should really get to school, because we're late."

Isaiah nodded and proceeded to the student parking lot and we both went inside the school. The entire time I was walking into the school, I thought about how he knew what was going on with me. Even though he didn't give any specifics, he still shocked me that he knew my business without anyone telling him anything. I figured I had overthought it, so I decided to think about how I was going to approach Scoop so we could be friends again. It had only been a week, but it had been a long one. Ultimately, I decided against it. If he wanted to still be friends, he could approach me first.

I walked into the cafeteria and collected my lunch tray. As I moved through the line, I eyed the special of the day that I held in my hands: grilled chicken breast, mashed potatoes with brown gravy, broccoli, and mixed fruit. I walked out of the line and zoned out to think of my life without Scoop.

I saw Isaiah and Malcom sitting together with three other kids, so I decided to go sit with them. I decided I wasn't going to sit alone this week. When I sat down everyone greeted me and continued their separate conversations. I chomped at my food because I was starving. If I was going to start over, I needed to become more outgoing and talk to people. That meant talking with people that had the same interests that I had. As difficult as the thought was to me, there was a door already opened with Malcom and Isaiah. Since we had started talking the week before, I figured I continue.

"So, have you started packing for this Northern Lights trip yet?" Malcom leaned over and whispered to me.

"No. I don't know if I want to go anymore. Unless you want to be my roommate because Scoop still isn't talking to me."

"Why not? Is It because of the argument you and Scoop got into? I know y'all not still on that. If that's the reason why you're not trying to go, then you need to get over that. Look, Scoop is in line and when he gets his lunch you need to talk to him because this is stupid." Malcom explained.

"If he wants to come over here then that's on him. Wait, how did you know we got into a fight?" I questioned with a confused look on my face.

"You and Scoop talk to each other every day. It wasn't hard to put two and two together."

Scoop gathered his lunch and saw Malcom waving him over to the table. He didn't see me or Isaiah at the table or else he wouldn't have come over. I held my head down as if I was more interested in my lunch than who was around me. Isaiah sat right across from Malcom while I sat right next to Malcom. Scoop sat down next to Isaiah unknowingly.

"What's going on people?" Scoop greeted the table with joy. I saw him glance at me and continue about his business.

"Scoop, you and J started packing for the Northern Lights trip yet?" Malcom asked.

"I'm already finished packing. I'm too ready to go on this trip. I'm about to borrow my dad's camera and record the whole trip. I am not lying when I say it's about to go down!" Scoop exclaimed with excitement. "So, me and you are going to be roommates, right, Malcom? Because I need to get inside information from you about your pops because my dad is a huge fan."

I lifted my head from the table in disbelief because I was supposed to be his roommate. I wasn't mad when Scoop blatantly ignored me, I gave a slight smirk of disgust and rolled my eyes. When Scoop saw my face, he looked at me with a blank stare and started eating his fruit like I was a stranger. I considered not saying anything the whole time, but I wanted to see what was really on Scoop's mind.

"Yo, are you still mad over that petty argument? I think it was stupid, and you should get over it. You said some dumb stuff, and I said some dumb stuff. I think this whole thing we got going on should be squashed right?"

Scoop was in the middle of a bite, so he hurried up and chewed before he spoke. He had his hand up with his index finger pointed up as a slight smirk formed on his face.

"I almost choked on that B.S. apology, my bad. But you know what, it's all good we can still go on the trip together. I just need some time with the future NFL pro sitting next to you."

I could tell when Scoop was being serious or sarcastic. This time, I was unsure, I decided to let it slide. I looked at Isaiah and he was sitting quietly enjoying his lunch, acting like nothing happened. He sparked a conversation with the kid next to him as he sat next to Scoop as if nothing had happened. Isaiah glanced at me, and he decided to say something.

"So, when are we going to meet to get this plan together for this trip? We need to talk about who's going to bring which snacks, what clothes to bring, and which system everybody will catch these L's on 2K."

The table erupted with laughter and banter. One thing to never do is bring up 2K with a group of boys. It was a way of life for most high school kids. I heard of kids having weekend tournaments for money. Arguments and even fist fights broke out because of the drama of the competitiveness. I heard of a story of two best friends fighting in front of their house because of the trash talk. They're still not friends to this day. Most of the violence and gambling happened at Tech on the North side of the city. While everyone at the table argued back and forth about who is the best at the game, I tried to decipher the mixed signal Scoop threw at me before that conversation came about. I pondered that as the rest of the boys argued their case.

When lunch ended, everyone laughed their way to their next class. Mr. P's class dragged by until the final period when I had gym. I was lucky to have gym, so I could let off some steam. Coach Limpsky was the gym teacher and everyone loved his class. I was a fan of gym because I was pretty athletic, but I never tried out for any of the sports teams. I would rather write than run or jump. We were playing dodgeball, so I thought throwing as hard as I could would make me feel better.

Coach Limpsky numbered all of us by ones and twos. I saw that most of the kids that were nerds were on the other team, and I had all the athletic kids on my team. So, this would be a piece of cake. We all lined up on the baseline on each side of the gym, waiting for the count down. When Coach ended the count down from ten all the way to one, we darted to the middle of the court and scrambled to grab the dodge balls as quickly as possible.

I was up against poor competition, so I was able to outrun most of the other team. I grabbed my ball and quickly back pedaled into a safe location and started scanning to choose my target. I found my first victim, and I launched the ball with everything I had. I nailed him right in the chest. His reflexes weren't quick enough. As I saw the kid I put out walk to the sideline, I saw in my peripheral a kid winding up to throw her ball at me. As I locked in on her, she released a sluggish throw that anyone could see a mile away. As I caught the ball and put her out, I was already in locate mode— as if I was in a stealth operation trying to eliminate the target.

I saw the perfect target, and she was standing near the right side three-point line on the opposite end. That was the same girl I seen twice before. Normally, she didn't have gym for the last period of the day together. I stared at her because she was just as beautiful as when I last lay my eyes on her. I drifted into an episode of daydreaming in the middle of the court. I envisioned walking on the beach while the sun grinned on our skin. I felt the crunch of the sand between my toes as we strolled across the shoreline. The cool air circulated through our noses as we took in the most valuable possession we had. Everything was perfect in my mind when I thought about her. She had beautiful light brown skin, curly black hair, penetrating hazel eyes, and a smile that should be displayed on a commercial.

As I continued to drift deeper into my imagination, the next thing I knew, a swift red dodge ball darted directly at my face at 100 miles per hour. I was hit so hard that I bit my tongue to the point where it bled. I flipped my locs behind my head as I held my hand under my jaw to keep the blood from dripping on the hardwood. Coach Limpsky ran over to me to make sure I was alright.

"You took quite a licking there buddy, maybe you should go to the nurse's office to get that looked at. Here, hold this towel to your tongue and I'll send someone with you. Hopefully you don't need stitches."

"I'll take him since I hit him. It is the least I can do," the voice said. I turned around to see who that was, and it was the girl I had been seeing the last few days.

She jogged over to me and rubbed my shoulder and said, "I am so sorry, I didn't mean to throw the ball at you that hard. You were such an easy target because you were standing there. Let me make sure you get to the nurse's office all right."

"Tamar, I guess that All-American arm is getting ready for the season huh?" Coach Limpsky said. "Class is almost over so you can stay with him until school is out. Make sure you all change before you get to the office. You can meet each other at the entrance of the gym."

I didn't say anything to either of them. I nodded my head yes and proceeded to the locker room, hiding my boyish grin beneath the towel. As I walked into the locker room, I couldn't contain my excitement because I had found out her name. Millions of thoughts streaked through my mind. What should I talk to her about? What is her favorite movie, does she like Pepsi or Coke, who is her favorite singer or rapper, Lebron or Kobe? The thing was, I knew how to talk to girls because I'm not an idiot, I just didn't know how to talk to the girl I had a crush on. The thoughts I had blocked me from concentrating on opening my locker. My combination was 13-24-23. I finally fumbled through the numbers to open it and put my uniform over my gym clothes because I didn't want to waste any time with Tamar. I loved saying her name because Tamar had a nice ring to it.

I lightly skipped out of the locker room to the gym entrance and game-planned my attack. I assumed I would start off by asking about her class schedule and then ask her if her and Scoop knew each other. Although Scoop and I were not in a great place, I knew I could always use him in small talk because everyone in our class knew who loudmouth Scoop was. Then I would talk about the Northern Light Trip after the small talk was out of the way, eventually getting to the point if she would like to hang out. I had everything set from start to finish.

One thing I knew was, I had to control the conversation because girls love a guy that can control things. I was bad at controlling things in my life to this point. I couldn't control who I lived with, I couldn't control keeping my best friend, and it seemed like I couldn't control what happened to me because I always got lost in my own thoughts. Thus, the bloody tongue that I received. I don't know what happened to me, but I think the rain from earlier and getting hit in the face was the wakeup call I needed. It was time to take control. I saw Tamar walking toward me as she turned the corner.

I practiced saying her name quietly to myself before she approached me.

"Thammoa, Thammaraa."

I couldn't even speak. My tongue was sore, bloody, and swollen. I'd thought about everything I needed except the importance of talking right. I gathered my thoughts quickly as Tamar sashayed toward me.

"Hey...um, you have a little blood on your tie," Tamar pointed out. "Here, I have wet wipes in my purse to clean you up a little bit."

"Phank you," I fumbled through trying to respond as I slightly bit down on my bottom lip to speak. She was even more beautiful up close. She smelled exactly how I thought she would. I had to catch myself before I slipped off into my own thoughts again. That's what got me in this situation in the first place. I shook myself and started walking with Tamar to the nurse's office. There was an awkward silence for fifteen seconds before she started talking to me.

"So, are you going on the Northern Lights trip in a few weeks?" I nodded my head yes as I switched from a bloody towel to a wet wipe she gave me. Tamar gave a quick snicker and said, "I must have knocked you pretty hard for you to not be able to talk. Let me see the damage."

I took the wet wipe off my tongue and stuck my tongue out as far as both of us could see. It was a deep cut. I couldn't see the whole thing so I pulled my phone out of my pocket and gave it to Tamar so she could take a picture of it. She paused for a split second before she took the snapshot and turned my phone around so I could see it. It looked like a gorge. My face scrunched up in disgust at what I saw.

"If you need stitches or anything, my dad will pay for it. I feel so bad, I am so sorry. I usually don't have gym my last period. I was bored and I didn't want to sit in study hall today." As I was flipping the wipe to the clean side, Tamar asked, "So you and Gary are friends? I know you might think I am weird, but I saw a picture of you both in your phone before I took the picture. The reason I know that is because my next-door neighbor likes him. I know you know who Tiffany Berkman is. Just don't tell him because I told her I wouldn't say anything."

In amazement and shock, I placed my hand over my gaping mouth. I didn't believe it when Scoop told me about her at the bus stop. I then did the zipper motion over my mouth then pointed at my tongue as if I was saying I couldn't talk anyways. We both giggled our way into the nurse's office. The nurse cleaned my tongue and patched me up. It was painful, but I couldn't let Tamar see my pain because she stayed with me the whole time. The nurse finished up as soon as the bell rang.

Luckily, I didn't need stitches. I had gotten a better grip on talking since my tongue was temporarily fixed. As we started walking through the crowds of students toward the exit, I became comfortable and bold enough to ask her a question.

"You know, we should sit together on the bus for the trip...with our friends, of course."

"Yea, I think that will be a good idea."

A voice yelled out to Tamar. It was one of her friends with a group of girls waving her over.

"Well, that's my ride. It was nice meeting and talking to you. I think I will introduce you to my brother, I think you would make good friends. He's going on the trip too. I will hook you guys up tomorrow if that is fine with you?"

I smile from ear to ear.

"I'm fine with that. Thank you and see you tomorrow. Thanks!"

She smiled back and twiddled her fingers goodbye. I was the luckiest kid on the planet. I didn't care about what happened with me and Scoop. I didn't care that I had to take care of B, I didn't care that I my parents were gone. My mind was fixed on Tamar, and I couldn't get enough of thinking about her. The boldness that had risen up within me wasn't the boldness I had when B fell down the stairs. It was greater because it was more controlled. I liked this version of myself because I was able to control something for once. I teetered on the idea of being more assertive a couple times in the past but maybe my bloody tongue was the starting point of something new. I had to bite my tongue for me to not bite it ever again. Up until this point, I felt as if life was predictable, and there was nothing I could do to change it. Life was a strain. I saw the new beginning through a knock to the head and a busted tongue.

I liked me.

I turned around and headed toward my bus. I walked to my usual spot, but suddenly I felt disgusted to sit there. That was a seat of self-loathing and deprivation. If I were to sit there, everything would unravel all over again. I decided to sit in the front of the bus. No more assigning myself to what the world wanted me to because it was time for me to make my own destiny. Some would say it is only a bus seat, why all the drama? It was more than just a seat for me, it was a decision on changing my life, and it had to start with one small decision. I sat down in the back of the bus and looked out the window and thought of how different my life was going to be with my newfound attitude on life.

I'd graduate high school and go to any college of my choosing. I'd be very successful in my writing and make millions of dollars traveling the world, talking about the joys of writing. I'd have a beautiful wife, preferably Tamar, with kids running around everywhere. We would live a lavish life free of drama and care. Today was the first step. I was so caught up in my own thoughts again, I didn't see Scoop come sit right next to me until he started talking.

"Ok," Scoop said sighing, "I said some stuff I shouldn't have said, and you did too, so I forgive you and you forgive me, cool? Cool. So, what is this business about you and Tamar going on the Northern Lights trip together? And since when did you start talking to girls? I was starting to think you were gay but no judgement here, you would still be my boy though."

Usually Scoop never apologized to anyone, including me when we had disagreements on small issues. He would usually brush it off and keep going, but I think the week-long silence hurt him worse than it hurt me. Either way, I was excited to have my friend back, it was boring. I smiled outside the window before I prepared my answer for Scoop.

"Um, I think someone spiked your drink at lunch because you are tripping right now. Before we get to that, are you and Isaiah cool again because he didn't seem like he was all that mad at you when he picked me up for school?"

"Oh, yeah, we talked last period we're cool. I told him that I was tripping because I was stressed about a test. We made a deal for me to go to his youth group after we get back from the trip. Oh, and by the way, you have to come too."

"Wait how did I get dragged into your little deal? Ugh, well anyways, to answer your question, I got a busted mouth in gym today, and Tamar volunteered to take me to the nurse's office because it was a pretty bad cut. I started leaking blood from my tongue. I don't know if you can see the cuts now but take a look."

I opened my mouth and stuck my tongue out for him to look at it. He cringed his face and laughed at me. I didn't want to tell him that she was the one that did the damage because I knew how he would react. We laughed and caught up from the week that we missed all the way to his house. I was so excited about my new beginning. I was glad my friendship stayed the same with Gary, He's the constant that I need.

CHAPTER FIVE

Hitch A Ride

The bus was at its final stop in our neighborhood, and we headed over to Scoops house. I loved going over there because his mom and dad were fun to be around. They were the typical parents I imagined having. They would tell jokes, have game nights, go to movies, and go on vacations. Scoop's little brother Todd was ten and the twins, Jamal and Jamarrah were five. Todd would always try and stay around us when we would be in Scoop's room. He was a cool little guy, though. On occasion, we would let him to tag along on some things that we did. When Scoop unlocked the front door, we walked into the living room where his dad was getting ready to go to the police station for his shift.

"Hey, dad, what's up?" Scoop said as we galloped toward his room.

"Yo, yo, slow down, fellas. What do y'all got going on today?" his dad asked.

"Nothing. We are going to play the game for a little bit and get everything together for this trip. Speaking of the trip, how much money did you plan on giving me since I'll be gone for a week."

"Money? Give? Trip? What do these three words have in common Scoop?"

"Um, they all involve me?"

"Yes, they all do involve you with one important part missing. You know what that is?" Scoop shook his head no. "The missing part is you don't have or will have any of them." Scoop's jaw dropped and he immediately changed demeanors from excited to irritated.

"But dad—" Scoop sighed in disbelief. Before he could finish his plea, his dad chimed in.

"Naw, I'm playing son I got you. I have $150 in an envelope waiting for you in the mail drawer. You should have seen the look on your face. Talk about priceless." I busted out laughing.

"Ha ha ha, very funny, guys," Scoop smirked. Mr. Rockland was a jokester. He always played little pranks on Scoop, and they would always get a good laugh out of it. In my neighborhood, a father being in the house was rare. What they had is what every Black kid my age lacked. Scoop and his dad were envied by everyone because they wanted what the Rocklands had. My dad and I didn't have a relationship. The last time I talked to him was right before I came to B's house. I thought one day he will be out and we could begin to bond.

"Dad before you head to work, could I get an extra fifty to make it an even $200? I want to get a new hoodie before I go because you know I gotta represent the Lakers."

"Lakers? You do know you live in Wisconsin, right? I don't think I raised you right because we're Bucks fans in this house. Well, I'll tell you what, you go out there and clean that garage, then that $50 is yours. And James, if want to help you out, there's $50 waiting for you too." I looked at Scoop, and he looked at me, we both said yes at the same exact time.

"Great. So, when that is done, let me know and I will give you the money. Man, you guys remind me of me and my friend back in the day. You couldn't separate us until we decided to be knuckleheads. Eventually, I wanted a better life than just trying to have fun and joined the Army, but he couldn't leave that life alone. When I left for basic training, we lost touch. I heard he's been in jail ever since. He was the best friend that I ever had. Just remember, stay brothers no matter what happens, stay out of trouble, and don't let a girl get in between you two. I saw many friendships and brotherhoods end because of petty arguments. But I know I can talk your ears off so let me get on to work. Scoop, your mom should be home in a few minutes. Watch your brothers and sister."

He walked to the door and turned the handle to leave.

He turned around and said with a big grin, "Have fun with the garage."

He shut the door and left. Immediately, we ran toward the back of the house and opened the garage. The door lifted and revealed Mount Everest. Boxes, old bikes, gym equipment, power tools and so much more stuff consumed the space. I knew what Scoop was thinking, and he knew what I was thinking, so we laughed in sync before getting to work.

Day after day for two and a half weeks after school, we would make our way through the garage like mad men on a mission. There were black garbage bags filled with useless papers and trash. Occasionally, Scoop's dad would watch us through the window while his mom would bring us bottles of water. We finally reached the back of the garage and we found some old Kodak cameras.

"Hey, my dad told me about some of the pictures on these cameras. We should go get them printed because I want to see what's on them. But where do we go to get these printed?" I shrugged in uncertainty, and we both decided to go inside and ask his parents.

"Hey dad, are these the cameras you were talking about a little while ago?"

"Whoa, you guys actually found them? I thought these were thrown away or something. Go down to the drug store and get these developed."

We ran there as fast as we could. It wasn't that far away from our house. It was a fifteen-minute walk. We waltzed into the store and marched to the photo counter.

"I can't wait to see what's on these cameras," anxiously Scoop said. "When my dad was talking about them, he made it seem like it was some wild stuff on there. A bunch of his friends went to Miami for their graduation trip, and there were some bad chicks."

"Man, you nasty, bro! I already know what you got planned for those pictures," I joked.

"Hello young men, what can I do for you," the employee asked.

"We would like to get these printed please."

"Ok, I can do that for you. They will be ready in about an hour."

"Great, thank you! J, lets grab some chips and we can wait outside on the bench until they're done."

We went to the snack isle and got as many snacks as we could buy and went to the counter to check out. We laughed and joked all the way up to the register. Just the thought of all the stuff we would see amused our imagination. The woman at the register looked like she was having a rough day. I looked into her eyes, and they looked tired. But when she locked in on us, she livened up a little bit as we approached her. We put our items on the counter as she scanned each one. She never looked down at all, only kept staring at us. We thought nothing of it.

"$16.19," she said with a slight attitude.

"Hey J, you pay because I have to get the pictures later." I reached into my back pocket to get B's debit card, but it slipped out of my hand and it fell to the ground. I bent over to pick it up and as I got back up and looked toward the register, the woman had her neck out over the counter, looking as if I was trying to get over on her. I continued to go about my business and proceeded to pay. As the payment went through, she snatched the receipt from the machine and slapped it on the countertop next to the gum and mints.

Scoop gave me a confused looked at the cashier and asked,

"May we have a bag please?"

The woman did not want to put our snacks in a bag. She rolled her eyes in annoyance and shoved our snacks in the bag and slung it toward us. She didn't give us a "thank you" or "have a great day," let alone a smile. We walk out of the store and sat on the bench that was connected to the building.

"Was it me, or was that lady tripping," I asked Scoop.

"She definitely was acting weird. We didn't even do anything. Oh well. Anyways, we got three days until Northern Lights. You ready?"

"I'm as ready as I can be. I can't wait to go. I'm nervous but excited all at the same time. You have to get a girl because you can't be third wheeling with me and Tamar. I'll see if she has a friend for you." I didn't want to tell Scoop about Tiffany because Tamar told me about her in confidence. I decided not to tell Scoop, even though I knew him longer that one class period.

"I'm a one-woman man. Me and Tiffany have something special. It doesn't matter to me that she's a senior and is going to college next year. She won't be able to resist all of this. Especially when I grow into my body all the way. You see how big my dad is, right? I'll be built just like that, but I won't be a police officer, I'll be a light heavyweight champ."

"Well, my bad," I replied with a smile. "I forgot that you are the champ. But on a serious note, I'm nervous about Tamar though. I never really talked to girls like that. I just go through so much on a daily basis, I really didn't really have the mind to have a girlfriend. Now that things are better with B, I'm starting to feel like a normal teenager. This is like a culture shock to me."

"Don't trip man. I think you will be fine. We're fifteen going on sixteen right now. The bad stuff we have going on right now will not last forever. Let's look at it this way, we're at a great school despite the neighborhood we live in, we have an opportunity to better our lives, and youth is on our side. Let the chips fall where they may."

"Scoop," I asked with concern, "you sound like your dad. Did he give you that speech?"

"Absolutely he did. You think I'm smart enough to come up with that myself? I told you I want to be a boxer, not a scholar. Boxers are typically not that smart. Besides all the hits we take to the head, how could we possibly remember anything other than get out of the way." I looked at the ground and thought to myself he does have a point. At that moment, a police officer was walking toward us gingerly.

"What's going on guys? What are you up to?" the officer asked.

"We are waiting to get out pictures back."

"You boys don't have smart phones? What you know about developing pictures? You know what," he interrupted me before I could answer him. "Do you guys have your ids on you?"

"I need to call my dad before I can give you anything. He's an officer," Scoop replied.

"I don't care who you dad is. He didn't teach you to obey an officer when they request identification from you? Give me your identification." At that point, I could see the officer inching toward his belt line. I saw this movie way too many times. So, I gradually started to put my hands in the air. But Scoop had always been a hot head and since his dad was a sergeant, he thought he had the upper hand in this fight.

"Look sir," Scoop said with an obvious attitude, "We don't even know why you are doing this to us right now. There isn't a no loitering sign, we're waiting here for our pictures, sir. Can we do that?"

"If you must know, there has been a report of a theft from this store. It just so happens that you two are here after I received the call. If you are cool, I will let you go, but if not, you may have to hitch a ride with me. So again, let's see those ids." The officer's stance had gotten more aggressive as him and Scoop exchanged words. I wanted this to be over quickly, so with the new outspoken me urging me, I spoke up.

"Sir, I would like to go home because I have a school trip I want to go on, and I don't want anything to cause me to miss it. Can I slowly reach in my pocket and get my id out? As a matter of fact, you can reach in my pocket and get it yourself."

I thought I was doing the right thing. I didn't have drugs on me, I didn't have any weapons, and I didn't steal anything. I had nothing to lose because I was clean. According to Scoop, I was wrong.

"J, don't you ever consent to a search man. You're a minor. You have the right to shut up and call a guardian. See, I hate officers like you. All you do is come to neighborhoods like this and terrorize Black people. But you know what, it is not your fault all the way. You don't know the culture, or the people, and you are expected to police the people you know nothing about. I bet you were a power-hungry white boy who was bullied in school. Those are the type of people who kill Black men for no reason. So, like I said, I am reaching into my pocket to call my dad who's a sergeant."

At the moment scoop started to reach in his pocket, the officer quickly reached into his holster and pulled out his gun.

He charged at Scoop with his gun pointed directly between his eyes.

"Put your hands where I can see them!" Scoop immediately dropped his phone on the ground. I thought he was going to be another notch on the belt of the police. The headline flashed before my eyes, *Unarmed Black teen killed by police officer.* I stood frozen in fear. As the officer approached Scoop, he holstered his gun and grabbed Scoop by the neck and took him down to the ground with his phone under his body. The look on the officer's eyes was of rage and anger. I saw the blood-filled vein pop out of his neck as he strained to keep Scoop's face on the ground. Scoop screeched in pain and squirmed to get out of the uncomfortable position. Anyone could see that they were in something more than an uncomfortable situation, especially my friend. I looked out of the corner of my eye and I saw the woman who checked us out of the store. She had this sinister look on her face as if Scoop was getting exactly what he deserved. At this point, I felt outraged. I knew she was the one who called the police on us. The same emotion came over me as when B had her accident, and when Scoop and I got into it. The only difference was that I controlled that anger I had, and I wanted to take my words and unload them on the woman. I walked near the automatic sliding door of the store and stood right in the middle so they wouldn't close.

"Listen lady, I know you called the police. We ain't do nothing wrong. The only reason why you did that was because you saw two black kids and got scared. It's people like you that make us look bad for no reason."

I was controlled in what I wanted to say. I was direct but I chose my words carefully. It felt good. The woman glared through my soul. Her eyes were telling a story that I heard about before. It didn't matter to me. I wanted to give that woman a piece of my mind. I heard the officer and Scoop struggling in the background. I stared at the cashier and she started to say something.

"Listen here you little—"

"Boy! You get down on the ground," the officer shouted at me with his knee in the back of Scoop while pointing the gun at me. "Requesting immediate back up at the corner of 14th and 75th."

I laid on the ground with my hand behind my head as fast as I could move. I heard sirens in the background as it grew louder the closer it came. I closed my eyes and imagined myself in the back of the squad car, hightailing it to jail. Having grown men look at my naked body as the guards strip search me. Being in the cell with men twice my age looking for a piece of me violently or sexually. The possibility of being in the same place my dad was in and becoming like him all started to seem like a reality I was headed toward. I guessed the relationship I wanted with my dad would actually happen, but the downside of that was we would both be in cages. With my eyes closed and tears running down my face, I felt a big hand grab my arm and snatch me up in the air. I thought this was it. I awaited the cold steel handcuffs to surround my wrists. I had in my mind to not resist and do exactly what the officer instructed. I opened one eye after the other, and Scoop's dad looked at me with great concern. I shook myself and finally surveyed the parking lot. The officer and the cashier were talking with the other officers, explaining their ends of the story while Scoop was picking up his broken phone from the ground. I was so shaken at the thought that Scoop might die, and I would be in jail. Scoop ran over to his dad and jumped into his arms with scraped cheeks and a dirty face. I saw the pebbles dribbling down his face hitting the ground as he tried to gather himself.

"Dad, all I did was try to call you like you told me to, I swear! We didn't steal anything! Look, I have the receipt right here. We were just waiting on the pictures to be done, and that officer came and pulled out his gun. I didn't resist or nothing, dad, I promise."

Scoop was visibly shaken and afraid of what his dad would do to him. I could tell Mr. Rockland had a slew of emotions overtaking him. After he saw that Scoop had minor wounds, he stormed over to the officer who escalated the situation and grabbed him by the front of his uniform and lifted him up off of his feet, then threw him to the ground. Mr. Rockland stood over him, pointed at him, and yelled.

"That was my son you were about to arrest! You're lucky that I wasn't here earlier, Conners. You put these two kids in harm's way when they did absolutely nothing wrong! I know one thing, your body cam had better been on this whole time. I'll see you back at the station after you get this mess sorted out. By the way, our little meeting will not be good." Officer Conners shook his head in offended agreement and went to speak with the manager of the store.

"I'll take you fellas home and we can talk about it when we get there. James, is Ms. Bailey doing ok enough for us to talk to her about what happened?"

"No. She went out of town for the weekend." Mr. Rockland did not know about the accident B had before. I knew he was going to want to talk to her about what happened. I had to figure out what to tell him after the weekend passed. At this point, it really didn't matter to me because Scoop and I had almost gone to jail or worse been killed.

"Dad," Scoop said, "We still have to go back in and get the pictures. I'll go grab them really quick." Scoop ran into the store and came back with the photos.

"Let's go fellas, hop in the back seat and I will take you home. James, I'm sure you want to stay the weekend over by our house, so make sure you let Ms. Bailey know you are here."

"I'll let her know when we get to your house. I'm still a little shook at what happened back there." Scoop and I crawled into the backseat of his dad's squad car. I lifted my hands off the seat and saw my hands shaking. I was still scared, and my adrenaline was still pumping. The fact that we made it out alive was a miracle.

"I was scared for my life, man." Scoop fiddled around with the envelope of pictures. "I thought I was going to die. I was trying to call you, dad. I told him you were a sergeant and he didn't believe me. We were just sitting down having a good time and he escalated the situation without knowing facts." At that point Scoop started to slowly cry. I watched tear after tear stream down his face. His breathing was getting inconsistent as he started crying harder into his hands. I saw his dad looking disturbed through the rear-view mirror. "Why can't every officer be like you dad? Why are cops so evil?"

"I can't tell you son."

I always knew that my skin was a problem to some people. I would hear about Black men and women getting killed at traffic stops and parks for justifiable no reason. Some were even younger than me. With my dad being in jail, I wondered what got him there. Was it because he was black or was it because he fell into what society was telling him he was like a criminal? I was unsure but I was glad to see Mr. Rockland supported and believed us. If it was someone else, our story would have ended different.

We finally reached their house and Mr. Rockland had to leave to finish up with what happened at the store. Scoop and I waited until his dad left to get my clothes from my house. We walked in and ran past the living room straight into the basement. We didn't even notice B. I hurried and grabbed my clothes and sat on the edge of my bed while Scoop sat on the steps. I threw my body back onto the bed with my arms stretched out and said, "Yo, that was wild. I thought you were about to die."

"I'm not about to lie, I thought I was dead. As soon as I started reaching for my phone, I immediately regretted it because my dad told me about reaching in my pocket. I guess I panicked for a second. As soon as my dad finds out about that, I think I will be in big trouble."

"Naw, I wouldn't worry about it. I think he is just glad that nothing happened to us."

"I guess you're right," Scoop replied, "Just don't tell anybody I cried because I have a reputation to keep up. In fact, I can't have Tiffany thinking I'm a punk."

His humor lightened up the mood after a dark afternoon. After our laughing subsided, I said, "I hope you brought those pictures over here." Scoop pulled them out of his pocket like it was a samurai sword. We opened the envelope and browsed through the photos. There were pictures of half-naked women, alcohol, and old party pictures from way back in the late 90's and early 2000's. As we were enjoying the pictures, there was one that caught my eyes that Scoop put to the back of the pile quickly.

"Hold on man, I think I noticed someone in that one you put at the back. Let me see it." I grabbed the picture from the back of the pile, and I saw Mr. Rockland with his shirt off holding a cup of what I assumed to be beer and someone else that looked exactly like my dad.

"Scoop, I think my dad and your dad knew each other in high school. That is my dad right there!"

Scoop bucked his eyes wide in amazement, "Wait a minute let me see." He sees the same thing and his jaw dropped. "Man, this is crazy, how is it that our dads were friends and we are friends? That makes us brothers, right?"

"I'm sure we're not, brother, because my family is to too jacked up for me to be related to you." I became still. I don't know why I felt this stillness within me at this moment. It wasn't shock, anger, or complacency. It was pure stillness like everything stopped moving. What just happened to Scoop and me didn't matter, B didn't matter, and the Northern Lights didn't matter. I didn't know what to do with what I just saw. I packed my clothes for the weekend while Scoop looked at the remaining pictures. I made sure I didn't leave my notebook because I had to write.

March 10th The light of Darkness

Darkness is all over the world but never at the same time. Space is dark all around even though light to the world comes from the sun in space that shines. Darkness provides shade and cools when the light is too hot. That's why we got all that swag. Darkness soothes and stills you in the night but not a thief like they say. Darkness provides subtle elegance that never brags. Darkness is big and brash that transitions a new day in a matter of a minute. Darkness is where God's greatest idea of light originated. Darkness is the absence where light cannot duplicate it. There are so many shades of dark that if you thought it, you'd have to close your eyes and think in the dark to comprehend it. Darkness is beautiful why can't the stars understand it? They are busy shooting in the dark and you can't count them all if you tried. But the stars can't outnumber the amount of darkness that resides in the wallpaper of existence. The stars are programmed to shoot whenever they please. It's their purpose to shoot then fail to exist. The point is stars eventually fall and darkness is the canvas where they cannot eclipse.

CHAPTER SIX

Faded

The long weekend was over, and I was so excited to have a chance to see the Northern Lights. It had been three days since the run-in with the police. The morning of the of the trip, I left Scoop's house earlier so I could make sure I had everything. I lay in my bed in the basement fully clothed with my bags packed while I waited for the time to dwindle down, so Isaiah could pick up Scoop and me from my house. I was so eager to leave the city. Up until this point, I had never been away from B for any length of time since I first came to her house at ten.

I was due for a getaway.

The school planned to fly us from Milwaukee to Seattle then to Anchorage. We would stay there for the night then drive to Fairbanks and stay there for the rest of the week. I had hardly slept the night before. There were millions of thoughts that raced through my mind that I couldn't reconcile. I wanted to go see my dad and ask him millions of questions. How did him and Scoop's dad meet? How did he end up in jail? I never knew why he was locked up because no one ever told me, and I never wanted to ask. When I got back from the trip, I decided I would go and see him. I never had gotten any letters from him since he had been in jail. My memories of him began to fade because I seldomly saw him before he went in. I couldn't tell anyone what he was like only his face because I had found a picture of him and mom in my backpack.

It was 5:00 in the morning and we were supposed to meet at the school at 5:30 so we could leave for the airport for our 8:00 flight. I grabbed my phone from my pocket to see if Scoop texted me. As soon as I unlocked the phone, his text "Come to the door, I'm outside" came through. I smirked and raced to the back door. We shook hands and made our way to the kitchen.

"Yo, we are out of here. You don't understand how ready I am to get going," Scoop exclaimed.

"Bro, listen, all of this stress got me tense. This is what I needed for real. You know I haven't been away from B this long. I'm going to soak everything in. And the best part about it is that Tamar and I are about to hit it off something serious."

"You ain't about to do nothing but mess this up. Listen to me, I'll guide you through this whole week, so whenever you need a wingman holla at your boy."

"Wait," I questioned, "I thought you were trying to get with Tiffany?"

"There's no trying man. I already got her. Besides, what she doesn't know won't hurt her."

"That sounds like a bad idea but thanks? I guess?"

Isaiah sent Scoop a text saying he was outside. We scrambled to grab our bags and the rest of our belongings for the trip. I ran downstairs to double check I had all of the essentials.

"Scoop," I yelled, "Go and head out I have to grab my charger really quick."

I heard the door close behind Scoop as he headed to the car. I found the charger, so I galloped up the stairs to the front door to leave. As I turned around, I saw B's chair empty. I was completely confused. I thought she had been miraculously healed. That meant the devil was back to make my life a living hell again. I slowly walked from the front door to the living room. From the living room to the kitchen. Finally, from the kitchen to her room upstairs and I could not find her. I had thought I was going to have a stress-free and fun trip. I guess God liked playing funny jokes.

I decided to look in the bathroom. I saw an empty orange bottle of B's Vicodin. She lay in the tub with her bloodshot eyes and her skin, which was usually dirty brown, turned pale white and her chest was rising and falling quickly. I felt her skin, and it was cold as if her blood had stopped running through her veins. I remembered this moment from months before. I was still. I tussled with the feeling of remorse and empathy. From what I could remember, she never loved me, and she always drowned me with her anger. She suffocated me with hate and in that moment, I rested in deep sadness because she had no capability to love. I bent down next to the dingy tub I cleaned and hugged her. Compassion arrested my lips as I whispered.

"I'm sorry."

As vomit and foam poured out of her mouth, I dried my eyes and walked outside like nothing happened. I had visions of B dying in front of me before, but I took no joy in the true version. She treated me like I didn't deserve life, but I still felt sorry for her.

I jogged to the car with my belongings in hand and walked to the trunk to fasten my bags. Through the rear window I saw Malcom in the front seat with Isaiah driving, and Scoop was on the driver side of the backseat. To my luck, Tamar was sitting in the middle of the back seat. I had just possibly witnessed a death, and my crush would be staring me in the face. I wondered why she would be in the car with all of these guys. I knew that she was friends with Tiffany who liked Scoop for some odd reason, but she wasn't coming on this trip because she was a Senior and only Sophomores went on this trip. I forced myself to keep my cool and be as smooth as I could be.

There was barely enough space for my things in the trunk, so I had to move the other bags around to make them fit. As I moved the items, there was a pill bottle that had Malcom's dad name on it that fell out of his bag. I picked the bottle up and it had a faint yet distinctive smell. This was weed and high quality at that. It wasn't reggie at all. I knew the difference in the smell because in my neighborhood, they are connoisseurs. I put it back into his bag. I hoped that he wouldn't get caught because that would be bad, especially in an airport. I walked slowly to the front of the door even though it started to drizzle a little bit outside. Rain was the least of my worries at this point.

"Hey what's good everybody. Let's get going," I said.

"Yessir, I've been waiting to go for the longest," Malcom replied. "Trust me, I got some tricks up my sleeve this week. Just wait on it."

"I hope so," Scoop said with zeal, "because with the week J and I had, we need this as bad as anybody. Isn't that right J?"

Before I could answer, Scoop started to talk again.

"Because almost dying or going to jail was a trip in itself. When that officer had me on the ground, I just knew I was dead. I saw my boy J holding it down with the lady who called the police on us for no reason. Then the officer got him down while I was in cuffs. Eventually, my dad came, and he tore that rookie a new one." I knew Scoop was trying to make me look much better because Tamar was in the car. He was doing his wingman duties.

"Wait, that was you guys?" Isaiah inquired. "This whole time I didn't even know it was you. I thought it was some of those boys that was on the north side."

"Nope it was us," I said as I mysteriously glanced over my shoulder to see if Tamar was impressed on how I conducted myself. I felt her body weight lean in toward me when Scoop explained what happened. I took a mental note that she liked bad boys.

I wanted to know why she was in the car with us as we approached the school. Either way, we were making a connection, so far at least in my eyes. The atmosphere of the car ride seemed great with the excitement of being away from home for a week. I could tell that the Northern Lights would be good to me, barring any abnormal incidences.

We parked in the student parking lot, and there were three coach busses waiting for the large crowd of students to board. They had their backpacks, luggage, phones, and tablets. Some of them had pillows, blankets, hats, gloves, and scarfs. It was colder in Alaska than it was in Wisconsin, so most of the kids came prepared. The teachers and chaperones were taking head counts as the kids entered the bus. We got out of the car and went to the trunk to get our bags to go on the bus. I was the first one to the trunk, so I was passing out everybody's things. The last bags were Tamar's. I wanted to impress her, so I picked her bag up over my head and gently set it down on the ground. I lifted the bar so she could roll her bag to the bus.

"Thank you," she said and smiled at me while she stroked her curly hair behind her ear. "I know I packed a lot so that bag was kind of heavy."

"Don't worry about it. I think I handled it well enough not to break it." We both giggled as I closed the trunk. As soon as I turned around, I heard Tamar shriek as if she was scared for her life. I quickly turned around and looked at her with concern. She didn't seem like she was in pain or anything.

"What is it," I asked, "Did you forget something?"

"I think I left my charger at home. Hold on a second let me ask my brother really quick. Hey Isaiah, did you grab that extra charger on the counter at the house?"

"Yep, I got it. I knew you would forget it, so I put it in my bag."

"Thanks, little bro!"

I was shocked that they were brother and sister and so close in age. I figured that they were twins to be in the same grade. I was relieved and yet nervous all at the same time because I had just become friends with Isaiah not too long before this trip. Her family was loaded with money, knowledge and influence, and my family was dead and in jail. How could I possibly be compatible with her? I felt so small in her large world, and I barely knew her personally. What could possibly be in her future intimidated me because I felt like I didn't have a future that could equate to that. I didn't even know what I wanted to do after high school while her full ride guaranteed scholarship to Howard. I thought it would be best to not worry about the future and focus on what was going on right now. I figured I could deal with B, my dad, and my future after the trip. My focus was on fun and Tamar.

"Hey, how much older are you than Isaiah," I inquired.

"I'm literally three minutes older than him. We're fraternal twins not identical. I tell him all the time, the oldest gets the brains and the youngest gets the beauty, but in our case, I have both." She shrugged arrogantly. "So, I was thinking that you could be my travel buddy for this trip?"

I blushed with nervousness, so I pretended to tie my shoe. I bent down on my knee and smiled.

"I think Scoop wanted me to be with him, but I think he will be ok for this week. I think we all are on bus three. Everybody is on it, so it should be pretty dope."

"Yeah, let's go. I'll go get my girls. Wait for me there, ok?"

I nodded and waited in line for bus three. While I waited, I saw Scoop, Malcom, and Isaiah a few people ahead of me, laughing and waving me to come up.

"Man, we saw everything that went down. You know damn well your shoe didn't need to be tied. You basically got on Velcro

Skechers. I ain't know you was trying to smash the homie's sister though," Malcom said.

"Wait, you saw that? And for the record, I'm not trying to smash your sister Isaiah. I didn't even know. I barely know her." I stumbled over my words nervously because I didn't want Isaiah to be mad that I liked his sister.

"Don't mention it," Isaiah said, laughing. "She told me about you after she busted your lip. She talked about how she thought she had knocked your tooth out because you talked funny."

"This guy is whipped and he's not even in a relationship yet. Get a load of this looser," Scoop joked.

"Y'all niggas done yet? Can we just get on the bus please? By the way, Tamar wants to sit next to me so, Scoop, you're going to have to partner up with somebody else."

"Look! I told y'all he was going to say that. That's all right, I guess us fellas will have to be a threesome then."

We all looked at Scoop in disgust and burst out laughing. "Come on guys get your minds out of the gutter for once," Scoop said, "You know what? I am just going to get on this bus and get our seat ready."

Isaiah and Malcom followed Scoop to the middle of the bus. I turned and looked back at all the other kids laughing and horse playing with each other. It put a smile on my face because I saw what could possibly be. Life without worry or stress. When I scanned the crowd, I saw a glimmer of hope. A sea of teenaged kids sprinkled with shades of white, brown, and black. I felt hope and clarity for the first time since I could remember. The hope was I could possibly be something more than what this country had given me.

At school, hope was presented to all students to advance in whatever career path of their choosing. South Shore Prep was the quintessential construct America wished it was. At home it was different because there was no hope. I was in the prison of my neighborhood. Drugs and violence were pillars of that community. It was dark there because of the atmosphere, not the people. A community of under loved and overlooked people who are seen as natural born criminals, thugs, and maligned people. To me, South Shore and my neighborhood were the same. The only difference was perspective, and I was fortunate to know both.

I patiently waited for Tamar to enter the bus. I practiced in my mind what conversations to have. I was edgy because I had never spent this much time with a girl by myself. I told myself to keep my cool and just act natural. I had my firsthand both sides of me on the seat. I felt a layer of water tickling my fingers. I was so nervous that I saw my sweat had made prints on the seats, so I wiped them on my pants. As I looked out the window, I saw Tamar and her friends coming in the direction of the bus. The thought of putting my hand around her shoulders as we talked passed my mind. I thought that was a good idea at first, but I shot it down before I embarrassed myself by doing too much. Tamar had a pink sweater on that was as vibrant as her smile. The moment she got comfortable next to me, I heard the guys three seats behind and across the aisle heckling me. They were saying things like, "J got the juice now," and "niggas get girlfriends and don't know how to treat his friends anymore." I acted like I didn't hear them because I didn't want to mess the moment up.

"Tamar, I hope you don't hear those fools behind me. They just trying to embarrass me, but it ain't working."

Tamar laughed with her hand covering her face, "No, it's not. I know how boys are anyways, my family only breeds boys. That is except for me." We both chuckled at the dry humor. "So, I didn't know if you had a neck pillow for the plane ride, so I brought an extra one for you."

I never knew neck pillows existed, so I decided to play it off like I knew. "Oh, thank you, I was looking for one of these before we left." After my comment, I thought that I shouldn't lie again. I wanted to be sure not to build this relationship off of lies no matter how big or small.

"Attention students," a teacher announced at the front of the bus, "I need everyone quiet for just a moment. A few things before we get going to the airport. First things first, make sure you have your travel buddy with you at all times. We will be doing a head count right now and at the airport, so keep the same buddy throughout this whole trip. Once we count you, we will give you a yellow lanyard to distinguish you are with South Shore. There will be multiple schools at the airport going on the same trip, but they have a different connecting flight, so it is imperative we all stay together. After we check in and get to our gate, we will do another count. We will give you further instructions from there. Just a reminder, don't forget to take off your shoes, remove large electronics from your bags, and take out your cell phones at the security checkpoint to avoid any hold-ups. We already have your boarding passes and will be handing them to you en route to the airport. As soon as the bus closes its doors, then we will be on our way."

I was anxious. I looked back at the guys with enthusiasm and then double checked my bag to make sure I had everything.

Tamar sat near the aisle while she chatted with her girlfriends. I leaned my head against the window and saw through my peripheral fog forming on the glass. The rain was beating on the ground, and I observed puddles of water rippling in the potholes as the buses rode across them. I suddenly felt at ease. I wasn't sure if it was the comforting sounds of the rain or my anticipation for the trip. In the brief time I had to myself while Tamar talked with her friends and the guys joked with each other, I had the chance to reflect. New flames possibly being kindled with Tamar, old relationships being renewed with Scoop, and my newfound confidence were top priority. I thought maybe this feeling is what being a normal teenager was like. I made a pact with myself to never let life or any bad situation overtake me. I vowed to never let my demons get to me again. I didn't want to end up like B, on the brink of death with no hope in the world. The same pills I'd dreamt about taking, she took, and she was all alone in a pile of her own fluids. My vison I wanted for my life lay within my own power and not in a pill.

"Go ahead and talk to your new boo, girl," Tamar's friend tried to whisper. Tamar nodded and turned back toward me. Her body language bellowed confidence. Her sixteen-year-old self was as confident as someone who has experienced life before. I was determined to match her energy. I wanted to say something attractive to her, but I was uninformed in this field. I had to freestyle.

"You know, I don't even have your number yet. I think we should exchange numbers so we can text about school and stuff." I didn't know how stupid that sounded. The only class I ever had with her was gym, and there were no notes for that. Besides, she wasn't even supposed to be there.

"I don't suspect I'll be back in that gym class anymore because of you know what." She pointed at my mouth, gently trying not to offend me. "But I will give you my number just in case we get lost on this trip." Tamar reached in her back pocket and pulled out her phone that was enclosed in a pink case with glitter on the outside of it. "Just tell me your number, and I will shoot you a text so you can have mine."

Step one was complete. I didn't know what the steps were to start an intimate relationship, but so far, I thought it was going well. I took my phone out in anticipation while I gave her my number. I was looking over at her phone while she typed my number in her messages. I nervously tapped the face of my phone with my thumb while she completed the text.

"Ok," Tamar said, "I sent you a text."

"Let me see." My iPhone 9 was outdated compared to her iPhone 12, so it took slightly longer for me to get the text. "Got it." The text was a simple smile emoji. I decided to get a little daring in my approach. "What name should I save you as in my contacts? Do you have a nickname, or do you just like to be called Tamar?"

"Well, my mom and dad call me Tashay because my first name is Tamar and middle name is Lashay. When they would ask me to say my name, I would combine the two names. They've been calling me that since I can remember. My brother calls me dumb and my friends call me TLC because of my initials. So, when it comes to names, pick your poison, just don't follow in Isaiah's footsteps and call me dumb because I fight boys."

We chuckled.

The bus had hit a bump in the road and my phone had jumped out of my hand due to the impact. It slid into the middle of the aisle next to Tamar. She then leaned over and picked it up. She gazed at my lock screen and saw that it was an old picture of my mom. I reached out my hand and she gave my phone back to me. I put my head down and shoved it back into my pocket. I saw that she was hesitant to say something to me.

"That was an old picture of my mom."

"Yeah, I saw that. She's very pretty. Is she excited about you leaving today?"

"She died when I was a kid. I don't remember much about her except from stories my foster parent has told me." I knew she was going to try and get more information about my family. I decided to open up a little bit. "My dad is in prison over in Waupun. He won't get out until I'm twenty-five."

"I am so sorry. I didn't know,"

I saw her eyes faintly tear up while she hid herself wiping them away.

"It's crazy how people like me, who have both parents and live in a nice neighborhood have privilege while being black. Just saying privilege and black in the same sentence sounds crazy. Isaiah told me about your encounter with my family, and you see how 'picture perfect' we are. But what people don't know is that we have issues of our own." She looked away with shame painted on her face. I thought of pressing into that conversation on the specifics of their issues, but I knew that look of shame.

"If you want to talk about it, I think I could understand issues better than anyone."

There was a space of silence for about ten seconds after she nodded in agreement. I didn't want to push the dialog of family matters, so I decided to lighten up the mood.

"Have you ever been on a plane before?"

"Yeah, plenty of times. We travel a lot. How about you?"

"This is my first time. How bad is it?"

"It's not bad at all. The worst part is takeoff. Make sure you chew gum so your ears don't pop. Before we board the plane, we can buy some snacks and stuff."

"I think I'll wait until I get off the plane to eat. I don't want to get sick and throw everything up."

"Oh, you'll be fine. Usually, first timers' experience isn't that bad."

We finally approached our terminal at the airport. We rustled up our belongings with our bags in hand. The rise of anticipation and chatter filled the bus as we filed out. The teachers and chaperones handed out our boarding passes and we walked inside the airport. Everyone was walking orderly to check in their bags before running to the security check. I approached line to show my school id and my boarding pass. I took off my shoes and put my phone and wallet inside the bucket to be scanned.

"Yo, would they tackle me to the ground if I said got explosives in my pants because I gotta blow that bathroom up," Scoop whispered in my ear behind me jokingly.

"Come on man why you gotta play like that? You trying to get us arrested, again?" I replied.

"Can we get the line moving? Y'all holding up the line," Malcom chimed in.

"All right, I'm moving. Just make sure your phones and stuff are out of your bags." I went ahead and walked to the metal detector.

"Put your hands over your head and line your feet on the yellow footprints below you," the TSA officer commanded. After it scanned me, I heard the beep. "You're good to step over this way."

I walked over to the bins where my stuff was located and put my shoes back on, put my phone and wallet in my pocket. I checked my backpack to see if I had my notebook in there to write because I knew I would write a lot. I looked in every pocket in my bag and I drew no luck. I was pissed. My book was like a bible to me. I put my backpack on and stepped away to wait for everyone else to pass through security. I scanned the airport looking angry.

There was so much traffic going in and coming out. People were hugging, playing, laughing, and enjoying life. I saw businessmen and businesswomen pacing on the phone trying to reach their office. One man even missed his flight. I saw a family sprinting to their gate because they were running late. I sat down on one of the benches facing outside where I could see the airplanes taking off and landing. I was directly under a departure sign. I was mesmerized at the elegance of the process of flying. The amount of communication from the tower to the pilots had to be clear and concise from start to finish. The airplane carried hundreds of humans at 400 miles per hour thousands of feet in the air to get them from one place to another for hours at a time. There had to be a certain amount of gas and there had to be a certain weight in order for everything to balance correctly. A machine big and bulky as an airplane has to fight against mother nature's wind, rain, snow, and storms in a wide-open space that lands to safety. Surprisingly, it eased my nerves. Watching the flights gave me hope because I too had fought elements that I couldn't control. I made decisions to go certain routes for me to be safe. In a world that was so big, I felt as if I was too small to even matter. Yet, I made a safe landing every time because I became my own pilot.

"Hey, do you have your boarding pass?" a mysterious voice asked me.

"Oh my gosh! I think I left it in one of the bins over there."

"Nope, I have it here. I saw you leave it in your bin after you passed security. Please make sure you keep it on you at all times, please." One of the chaperones saved my life. I thought I was going to have to miss out.

"Bro, you are so dumb," Scoop announced, putting his boarding pass in his pocket. "You really need help, don't you?"

"Man, shut up. At least somebody was looking out for me unlike some people. That reminds me, I have to get a new notebook because I left mine at home."

Malcom wrapped both of us in each of his arms and began walking toward our gate. His expensive cologne smelled wonderful.

"Look fellas, let's go in the bathroom because I have to show you something," Malcom insisted like a car salesman.

We went in the bathroom in the handicap stall so there could be enough room for all of us to fit. He pulled out a three pill bottles of what looked like pain medication. He opened one bottle and pulled out the cotton balls and weed was at the bottom. This was the bottle I saw in the trunk. I had thought he would have been caught for sure.

"How in the hell did you get that through security," I asked in fear.

"Listen, a magician never tells his secrets but, I'll tell you. I took a few bottles of ibuprofen and emptied the pills for the weed. Then I put cotton balls on top of the weed and put the pills on the cotton ball. I knew I couldn't get past with aluminum foil, so I had to improvise."

Scoop's eyes squinted in curiosity. "Um, I just have a few questions. Number one, have you done this before? Number two, if so, how did you know it was going to work? Number three, I hope you have something to roll up with because I'm trying get lit in Alaska. Could you imagine being high and watching the Northern Lights, my nigga?"

"To answer your questions, no I haven't done it before, I knew it was going to work because my dad did it, and why would I not bring something to roll with, bro? That would be irresponsible of me."

"Excuse me, guys," I chimed in. "You know it would be impossible to do with all of these parents and teachers with us every day all day, right? And Scoop we don't even smoke so what you talking about rolling up? You know your dad would beat the breaks off of you if you got caught."

"Well, for your information lame of the year, this is a once in a lifetime experience. Why not live it up? Come on man it would only be one-time man. Loosen up bro. What my dad don't know won't hurt him."

I shook my head and walked out of the bathroom to find Tamar. I saw her come out of the bathroom at the same time I did. I didn't want anyone to find out about the activities Malcom and Scoop wanted to do so I kept my mouth shut.

"Hey, traveling buddy, did you want to go to the gift shop right now to get that gum?" Tamar asked.

"Sure, let's go."

We walked into the shop and saw t-shirts, hats, hoodies, shot glasses, and mugs all with Wisconsin on them. They even had teddy bears with t-shirts with the shape of Wisconsin on it. I didn't know people loved this state like that. I picked up a miniature basketball and signaled for Tamar to catch. I threw it and she caught it. It was my turn to catch it.

"I'm paying attention this time, so you don't have the chance to rip my tongue open again."

She laughed and floated the ball nicely. We got a good laugh out of that. We browsed around for a few more minutes and proceeded to the counter to check out. I put my gum and notebook on the counter and she put hers there as well. She tried to put lip gloss on the counter as well, but it rolled off onto the floor. We both bent down at the same time to pick it up. We touched hands on the floor. I pulled back quickly while we both awkwardly apologized for the moment. It seemed like a scene right out of a movie or romance novel. I brushed it off as if it was nothing. I hurried and pulled out B's debit card to pay for the few items.

"Oh no, James, you don't have to pay for my stuff."

"Don't worry about it. It's literally four things. If you want, I can let you get me a keychain in Alaska, deal?"

"Deal."

CHAPTER SEVEN

How High Are We?

"Attention, Delta flight DL1932 departure to Seattle, Washington for gate G14 is on time and will be boarding shortly. We will ask all passengers to be seated by zone number starting from zone 1 through zone 6. If you are military, SkyMiles Member, or have any children under the age of two you will be able to board first. Thank you for your cooperation and thank you for flying Delta Airlines."

"Which seat are you, Tamar?"

"I'm 13C. What about you?"

"I'm 18E."

"You know what, I'm sure we can get someone to change seats with us so we can sit together. Let me go talk to my girls really quick, and I'll meet you when they call our zone."

That was perfect because it gave me time to reconvene with Scoop and those guys. Tamar and I walked toward our gate and split up as soon as we approached our group. I saw Tamar's friends giggling as if they were trying to embarrass her. Their eyes darted back and forth between Tamar and me. It felt good to get that kind of attention. I walked up to where Malcolm, Isaiah, and Scoop were.

"Isaiah is going to end up smothering you if you keep flirting with his sister like that, ain't that right, bro?" Malcom insinuated as he nudged Isaiah with his elbow.

Isaiah laughed and said, "Look man I really don't care what she does. She is older than me, and if she wants to date then who am I to get in her way. I'm going to date too so who cares."

"Who do you got your eyes on at this school," Scoop asked.

"I'm going to wait to go to college to date because I am not trying to end up with a baby in high school. Our teenage hormones are running wild right now, so I don't want any slip ups going to Morehouse."

"I knew it. You're waiting to dip into some of that milk chocolate, huh? Blacker the berry the sweeter the juice. I knew church boy had something on him too. He's racist. You don't like people who aren't Black, do you?" Scoop folded his arms aggressively. I felt like Scoop didn't all the way squash that situation with Isaiah. It seemed like he was still a little bitter.

"First of all, Black people can't be racist because we do not hold enough power, at least in this country or in this school for that matter to marginalize any other group. I think the word you were looking for was prejudice in which I am not for reasons I will explain after my second point. Second of all, why is it when us black people want to be exclusive inside our race of people it is considered prejudice? I mean seriously, the Chinese people marry within their own race, the Mexicans, Indians, Natives, and others do the same. Does that mean I treat everyone else as less than? No. Does that mean I am not attracted to anyone outside of my race? No. That means I have a preference. I treat everyone I encounter, no matter their ethnicity or race, with the same dignity and respect I show a Black person."

"My nigga is batting 1000 right now against you, Scoop. How my man's come at you sideways in the nicest way possible," Malcom butted in, joking.

I said, "Scoop, your dad had that same conversation with you. You should know that. Isaiah is like a pastor, man, he can't be prejudice because that goes against what his religion says, I think."

"Yes, it does go against what I believe. The Bible talks about how there will be people from every nation and tongue worshipping Jesus. If I want to be a person like Jesus, I can't be prejudice against someone because they are a different culture or color."

"Delta flight DL1932 departure to Seattle, Washington will begin boarding. If you are military, SkyMiles Member, or have any children under the age of two you may begin boarding. Have your boarding pass ready as you approach the gate."

"I would love to keep this bible study going, but we do have a plane to catch," Malcom said. "Which zone are you guys? I'm in zone 3."

"I'm zone 3."

"Me too."

"Same here," I said. "Who has seat 13B or A because Tamar wants to sit by me?"

"I have 13A. I think they booked ours at the same time since we are siblings. I'll switch seats with you."

"So, J. When exactly are you going to hit?" Malcom asked. "Because I have to hit something on this trip. One of these little trust fund girls are going to get it. I don't care if she's pasty white or midnight black. I don't discriminate. We all the same color when the lights are off."

Scoop laughed and shook hands with Malcom in agreement and said, "You have never lied, bro. If Tiffany was on this trip, I would be doing the same thing J is doing."

"Oh my god, I am not trying to smash her! I don't even know her like that. And you don't think that's disrespectful to Isaiah to talk about his sister in that way? I mean have some decency, fellas." I had no intention to even think about having sex with Tamar. I didn't know what sex felt like. It wasn't like I never felt those feelings before, it was I was too busy trying to stay alive at home.

I knew Isaiah felt uncomfortable with that conversation, so I felt like I had to say something to deflect. Luckily, the woman at the gate called our zone, and Isaiah and I separated ourselves from Scoop and Malcom so they can horse around. We scanned our tickets at the front gate. I felt a tap on my shoulder as I was walking through the bridge to get on the plane. It was Tamar with a smile on her face.

"Hey, Zay, where are you sitting? I told James that I would sit by him on the way there. I think we are sitting together because of our names."

"Yeah, that's fine," Isaiah said. "We talked about it earlier so we can switch seats. I think everybody is going to move around anyways."

It seemed like they always got along. I never had a sibling to get along with. Scoop wasn't a sibling, but it was as close as I would get. I was always a loner but that was okay with me. I couldn't imagine what sort of trauma two kids would have to go through with a parent dead and another parent in jail. A promise I said I would keep to my children is to make sure I am an adult before I have kids. By that time, I would be in a good place with myself and essentially my wife. I would be twenty-eight with a great career preparing for them to come into this world. I wouldn't be in jail or dead but just your normal average Black American family.

We entered the front of the plane and the cockpit doors were open. The pilots were getting prepared for the flight. There were so many buttons and lights on the dash that it looked like a Christmas tree. There were two Black women that were the captain and co-captain. One of the women had long dreadlocks that were put up in a ponytail and the other woman had an afro. They both had a pin on their uniforms. I could barely see, but there were words on them. The only word I could make out before I turned the corner to walk down the aisle was Sigma. I knew it was a sorority, but I didn't know which one it was. I wasn't accustomed to flying, but I knew being a pilot was something Black women weren't historically apart of.

Tamar walked in front of me and escorted us to our seat. I grabbed her bag to put in the bin above us. I sat in seat A next to the window. I tightened my seatbelt and turned my phone on airplane mode. Flight one was about to start. Tamar was texting and getting last minute conversations out of the way. As the last passengers took their seats nervousness set in.

"Thank you for flying Delta airlines," the pilot spoke over the intercom. "We will be taxiing to the runway in just a few moments. We are looking at an arriving about ten minutes earlier than expected. We are looking at partly cloudy skies in Seattle with a few rain showers when we arrive. There will be a little turbulence upon arrival so make sure your seatbelt is securely fastened when the seatbelt sign is on. Once again, thank you for flying Delta airlines and enjoy your flight."

I tightened my seatbelt more against my waist. I wondered why would they only have seatbelt across our laps instead of our chest and lap? The airplane suddenly jerked to a stop. I didn't notice that we were already going to the runway. I pulled up the window shade and saw other planes take off one after another. We were next in line. I gripped the arm rest as tight as I could. The plane began to speed up as we started to takeoff.

"Hey, just relax. This is the worst part of the flight I promise. Once we get in the air, you won't even feel like you're moving."

Tamar then reached over and placed her open palm on my leg as if she was petitioning me to hold her hand. It worked. I slowly placed my hand inside of hers. It was a perfect fit. We didn't interlock fingers, but I didn't care about that. She was genuinely trying to comfort me.

The pressure began to weigh on my chest as the nose of the airplane lifted off of the runway. It felt like my body was glued to the seat as the elevation increased. I squeezed Tamar's hand a little tighter. The higher we went, the more I felt lightheaded. My ears started clogging and I could barely hear. I tried to pop my ears, but I had no luck. I saw Tamar looking at me out of the side of my eye. She reached into her pocket to grab something.

"Here, take this."

She gave me a piece of Winterfresh gum. I started chewing it and my ears slowly began to open up. When we got to cruising altitude, I started getting sleepy. I fought my eyelids to stay open, so I could get the full flight experience. Being in the air was peaceful. The blue skies and white clouds were euphoric. Once, this was territory untapped by humans since the beginning of time. It took people who wanted a new innovative way of transportation to change the trajectory of the way people lived. There were years of trial and error, crashing, and failed flight attempts. It took years of successful steps with unsuccessful back pedals. Eventually, the code was cracked. All it took was time. The process of flying is great with planes, helicopters, and jets, but I think it is only a scratch on the surface.

March 15th Travels

Floating is a dream to me. Like a cloud unburdened by the atmosphere. Billowing life rolls effortlessly. The wind carries me far and near. I've never seen this before. Shiny things breaking my stride. Its loud and I see the people adore. Being where I am surrounded by built supplies. I live off of what is given to me. I survive off of water you can't see. I'm formed by what's not seen by the naked eyes. Of the ones who prepare their life off of my cries. I cry so your spirits won't be broke. I cry to rise his seed unprovoked. Floating is a reality to me. I'm a cloud unburdened by the atmosphere. The life of a cloud rolls effortlessly. I go where I want, and I go far and near.

I closed my eyes and drifted to sleep.

I hear the cheers of thousands of people in what looks like an Olympic track. I'm at the starter's block in position to take off running. The starter pistol sounds off.

Pow!

I take off as fast as I can. After six good strides one of the fans throws garbage in the lane I was running in. I dodge the debris and keep my stride. I turn to round the bend and more people chuck popcorn, pizza, water bottles, and candy in my way. I stay as poised as I can as the wind rushes past my ears in route to the second turn. The race feels never ending, but I keep my pace. The second turn arrives and another coach throws a hurdle in my lane. I jump as best as I can. I don't make it over. I crash and land on my face. I feel the scrape on my right cheek as I lie in my misery. I am determined to finish. I push myself up and start sprinting. It feels like someone is gaining up on me, so I dig deeper in my will and give it everything I have. After the third lap around the track, I'm at the last 100 meters for the final go around. I move my legs as fast as they can move, but before I get to the finish line, I feel as if I start floating. My feet are moving on the ground, but my speed is as if I'm walking.

"We have started our initial decent into Seattle, Washington. Arrival time is 2:53pm. The temperature is currently at 52° with partly cloudy skies. We do ask that since the fasten seatbelt sign is on, you do remain in your seats with your seatbelt securely fastened. Flight attendants prepare for final decent. Thank you for flying Delta Airlines."

It was a dream. I couldn't believe that I slept throughout the whole flight. One down, and one more to go. I had no clue what that dream meant. I wasn't much of a dreamer, and I wanted to remember it so I wrote the details of it in my notebook. When I finished, Tamar woke up. I wasn't sure if my breath smelled because I was sleep so took a piece of my gum out of my pocket to chew it before I talked with anyone.

We landed and taxied to the gate we were supposed to get off.

"Students from South Shore, we will all meet right in front of the gate to we can get a head count on everyone," one teacher yelled out as passengers were getting their bags from the overhead compartment.

It was our turn to stand up and get our stuff. I made sure I got Tamar's bag down for her. We walked out of the airplane as the attendants and the captains bade us a farewell. I had a chance to look at the pilot's pins on their uniform and it said Sigma Gamma Rho.

Scoop and the guys met up with me, Tamar, and three of her friends at the gate while all the students and the chaperones gathered together until everyone was accounted for. We were led down to our last flight to get to Alaska. We had a little over an hour before we boarded our next flight. Malcom tapped my shoulder.

"Hey man, I heard you was snoring on the plane, bro."

"I was? I hope I wasn't too loud. Shit, now Tamar knows I snore."

"I'm playing man, I didn't hear you. You were knocked out though. Here I got these mini brownies from my house to keep you up. I already gave Scoop and Isaiah some. I brought enough for Tamar's lady friends too. A little quiet secret is I made them myself. Kind of a hidden talent of mine. If I don't make it to the NFL, I'll own my own bakery with a little twist."

I took a brownie and it is the best brownie I have ever tasted. So, I ate one after another, and another.

"Hold on, bro. You might want to slow up, man. Save some for the rest of us. See if Tamar and her girls wants in on these."

I asked Tamar and her friends if they wanted some and the accepted. They ate three each. I swear they swallowed them faster than I ate mine. Tamar's friend Ashley A wanted more, but Malcom was all out.

"Hey Malcom, have I ever told you how cute you were?" Ashley A asked.

"No, I don't have any more Ashley. But I do have something else that you will enjoy."

"What do you have in mind"

Malcom cunningly showed a rolled-up joint in his backpack.

"We can save this for the hotel. I don't want y'all too high before dinner tonight."

"Wait! What do you mean high?" Tamar said conspicuously.

"Shh! Come on now," Malcom said while he looked around as if all the attention was on him. "You trying to get a nigga locked up? I told you it had a little twist. Don't worry though. I didn't put too much in it though. I had this planned out for weeks. I was going to get y'all high regardless."

Isaiah chimed in, "Yo, man that was not cool, bro. You trying to get us all in trouble?"

"Man, stop tripping. You will be high for about two to three hours. That's about as long as this flight. Let's all chill and grab some food because I know you will be hungry in about ten min-utes anyways. It's crazy that Scoop is the only one that's down with the shits."

I was so shocked that I couldn't speak. I just went along with the plan. We bought chips, candy, donuts, pizza, and cheeseburgers. I wasn't scared for Malcom or Scoop, but I was for Isaiah and Tamar. They were like golden children that never did anything bad. Granted it was only weed, their dad was a pastor and if I was right about preachers, they would think down on people who got high. Especially if it was their own kids.

It had been about thirty minutes since we ate the brownies and we were laughing the whole time. My mouth was dry, so I went to the vending machine to get a Gatorade. I tried putting my dollar in the slot, but it would not go in. I flipped it around three or four times, and it wouldn't take. I got agitated. Scoop came to my aide.

"Bro. Can you tell me why you are trying to put the dollar in the coin slot?" Scoop laughed and pointed while everyone else followed suit.

"How high am I?"

CHAPTER EIGHT

It Just Got Real

Our shenanigans had only begun. It had felt as if I had floated on to the plane. I had never been high in my life, and my first experience of being high was my second flight. The flight to Anchorage was a blur. I was on cloud nine way before we were 30,000 feet in the air. The only thing I remembered was one of the teachers coming into the area where all us high kids were and scolded us for being too loud. Malcom said the high was going to go down in three hours, but my high stayed the same. Two of Tamar's friends decided they didn't want to be around Malcom anymore, so they buddied up with another group of students. That left Tamar and Ashley A as the only girls with our group.

After a long day of traveling, we had reservations at a hotel to stay for the night before a bus trip to Fairbanks the next day. It was supposed to be a blizzard north of where we were, but it would turn directions and not be in our line of travel.

The school had a policy that no boys would be sleeping in rooms with girls. There was a strict curfew to abide by. Every night that we were not out as a group, the curfew would be set at 9:00 and lights out at 10:30. There weren't enough chaperones for the groups of kids, so they wouldn't be able to monitor properly. That answered my question of how they could stop them from getting high. I thought being high was going to be a bad experience, but I started to like the feeling. We finally got on the bus and headed to the hotel. Instead of going out to dinner, we all voted for pizza. It was way too cold for us to go out as a group. Luckily, for us four boys, we didn't have a chaperone rooming with us, so when they had to check in on us, we horsed around until one of them would knock on our door to see how we were doing. Our pizza showed up and since we were boys, it didn't last long.

By the time we finished, it was 10:00. It was almost time for lights out, and I was still high. Malcom pulled out his joint and pointed to the bathroom. Scoop was the first person to agree while Isaiah declined.

"Yeah, you got me the first time, you won't get me again. Just to let you know, you can't do that to me again, man, for real. I don't mess with anybody and I try to stay in my lane. If you try that again we are going to have a problem. You're cool and all Malcom and I like you but there are some things that you just don't do."

"AHHHH!" Scoop pointed at Malcom and laughed while rolling around on the bed. "I was waiting for him to say something. I thought Isaiah was soft but it looks like he'll get down with anybody."

"Naw man, it's not even like that. I was always taught to never be scared of anybody and speak your piece no matter who it is."

"My bad, bro. I got you. You're cool people and I messed up." Malcom apologized while trying to light the joint. "But uh, J, you down to smoke this 'J'? It looks like you're still high from them edibles."

"Come on man we are in Alaska of all places," Scoop pleaded with a pizza stain on his lip. "B is not going to find out about it, man. Like I said, this is a once in a lifetime experience. If I really wanted to smoke weed, I would buy from them fools around the corner, man. You know that. Come on, let's just let loose a little bit. We smoke all week and once we get back to Wisconsin we'll go back to normal."

Peer pressure is a bitch.

We walked into the bathroom and ran the hot water in the shower so it could steam up. Malcom stuffed the hotel door and the bathroom door with towels so the smoke wouldn't seep out into the hallway. I was the first one to hit the joint first. I never smoked before and my lungs made sure to tell Scoop and Malcom that I was a novice as I coughed up the first puff I took. It felt like I wanted to cough up my lungs.

"Hey man it's all good for your first time. It happened to me too," Malcom reassured me once my coughing subsided. "When you puff the smoke in, hold it in and try to suck the smoke into your lungs for as long as you can hold your breath and then exhale as smooth as you can. You get a better high that way."

"Duly noted," I said as I took my second puff. I held the smoke in as long as I could and let the smoke fill my lungs. Another failed attempt as I coughed even harder the second time.

"Puff, puff, pass, bro!" Scoop said as he held his hand out to receive the joint.

He was excited to smoke. I don't think this was his first-time smoking because he didn't cough once. When his turn was done, he passed it to Malcom. He was a pro. The first hit he took, he had made a circle with the smoke he blew out. The second cloud of smoke he blew out of his mouth, into his nose, and back out of his mouth. There wasn't any wasted smoke. By this time, the bathroom was filled with a mixture of steam and smoke. The mirror had a thin layer of fog hovering on its surface. I couldn't see our reflections on it, but I think it was best that I didn't see what I looked like.

As ashamed I was to smoke, it was putting me into a space of euphoric emotion. I had never felt so free in my life. At this moment, I didn't care about anyone or anything. With every inhale of smoke, I felt an intense feeling of every emotion I had gathering into my mouth, traveling through my windpipe, and down into my lungs being withheld. As I held my breath, I visualized my past, present, and future in a matter of seconds. The exhale was the most tranquil feeling because I could breathe again. Holding my emotions, actions, and feelings in had hurt me for so many years. Just like I controlled my exhalation of the smoke, this felt like the culmination of my arrival. I don't believe it was the marijuana that did it, I think it was the meditation that did the trick. For years I laid on my bed letting my mind wander of what could be ahead of me without any direction. At this moment, with my eyes closed, I had control of the very thing I had lost control of. Tamar making me bleed was the thing that broke that shell, the officer refined me, and this smoke sealed it. Although I would never make smoking a lifestyle of mine, I was grateful for what that plant did for me.

We smoked until it was down to the nub. Malcom saved it for later when we would smoke again, he would take what was left inside of the wrap and put it in the next one. Exiting the bathroom, the smoke and steam mixture followed us out as if we were being tailed by ghosts. Isaiah looked up at us and laughed. It didn't feel like a laugh of judgment, but a laugh of understanding. There was something different about that kid. He seemed a little too perfect. I was feeling bold, so I decided to ask him a question.

"Isaiah, why didn't you come smoke with us? You were already high."

"Getting high isn't my thing."

"Is it because of your religion?"

"Well, yes and no. Everybody makes decisions on things that they think are right or wrong."

"Do you think smoking weed is a bad thing or a sin?"

"Well, I don't think it is a sin at all. Weed is a natural plant that has many health benefits. I think it can be abused just like other things. For example, the one thing that people don't really think that is abused is food. We need food to live, have energy, and function properly. There is nothing wrong about eating, but, when you start abusing food, that is when diseases come. Diabetes, high blood pressure, clogged arteries and the list goes on. I'm a firm believer of what the Bible says. In 1 Corinthians 6 it talks about being able to do anything you want to do, but not being under the power of it. I don't want to be brought under the power of anything."

"Yo, that is some deep shit," Malcom responded quietly but loud enough for us to hear. "So, your belief is like mastering your own environment? Kind of like Hinduism and Buddhism you know? Treat people right and good things will happen type stuff."

Isaiah chuckled. I knew he was going to give us one of his famous speeches. I was actually excited to hear exactly what he believed because religion was not my thing.

"Christianity is nothing like that. I'll give you the short version. I believe Jesus died for the sins of the world and rose from the dead and is now in heaven waiting to return to judge the world. Jesus said I am the way the truth and the light. No man comes to the Father except by me. To be saved, we must repent of our sins and confess said statements. Jesus gave us two commandments: Love God and love our neighbor. Both of which Jesus not only demonstrated but embodied. He embodied love and God because he is God."

"Wait I'm confused," Scoop questioned. "Is Jesus a guy or a God?"

"He's both."

"How sway!?"

There was a knock on the door along with a scolding, "Hey! What is going on in here?"

We all scrambled like roaches when the light is on. Malcom pulled out an air freshener to try and get the scent out.

"Nigga, this is not going to work." Scoop whispered as loud as he could without being obvious to the mystery man at the door. "Open the window."

Isaiah hurried and opened up the windows to get the faint smell of marijuana out.

"I got an idea, let's all pretend we were sleep. I'll go outside to 'get some ice' because I was thirsty, and I will close the door behind me to get rid of whoever that is." Isaiah suggested.

"Yeah, do that. I'll turn all of the lights out. We all gotta lay on opposite ends of each other because I am not trying to spoon one of you fools," Malcom said.

The lights were off, and Scoop and Malcom laid on opposite ends of the bed of each other to where they were smelling each other's feet. I jumped in the other bed and pretended to be asleep. Isaiah opened the door yawning and walked outside with the ice bucket in his hand. We stayed as quiet as possible while we waited for Isaiah to come back. Isaiah was pretty cool despite not wanting to smoke. He seemed like he was willing to help and not rat us out even though he had a good reason to. After a few minutes, the door opened, and Isaiah walked in and leaned on the door after he closed it.

"Man, that was close. Next time, you go outside and smoke." We laughed hysterically.

After a much-needed night's rest, we gathered our things to get ready for the drive to Fairbanks. We showered and cleaned ourselves up one-by-one and made our way down to the lobby for the breakfast the hotel had. It was a light breakfast of scrambled eggs, bacon, toast, bagels, orange juice, coffee, and cereal. There weren't many people eating yet because they were all still getting ready. It was 8:30 and we were scheduled to leave at 10. When we started packing our plates, other kids started coming into the breakfast area. They had on different colored lanyards, so I knew they weren't with our school.

"Hey, are you guys from Chicago?" one of the kids in the other group asked.

"Why do we have to be from Chicago? Why not just ask where are we from? Or are we even American?" Isaiah snapped back.

Scoop chimed in and said,

"Yeah, is it because we're Black we have to be from Chicago? Y'all gonna be straight up rude like that?"

The group of five students with blue lanyards on looked at each other as if we were the ones asking them out of line questions. One kid started to walk a little closer to us. He was a tall white kid who wreaked of privilege. There were kids who grew up with money that attended South Shore, but he was different. He looked like his dad was not only loaded with money, but with power as well. You could tell by the way he felt he could talk to us.

"Whoa, fellas," he said arrogantly with his hands up as if he was trying to de-escalate the situation. "I think we got off on the wrong foot. Maybe my friend here was a little forward in his questioning. I'm Conner and I think we should start over. My buddy didn't mean any harm with what he asked. We're from Orange County. No harm. As a peace treaty, we have something that we think will smooth everything over."

He pulled out a bag of mushrooms inconspicuously. I had just experienced being high the day before, but I did not want to start hallucinating on my second day. In the hood where I lived, the drugs of choice were marijuana, crack, and heroine. The white people drugs were mushrooms, meth, cocaine, and pills. I figured I'd stick with a normal high for the moment.

"Man, we don't do that," Malcom replied. "Now if you got some loud then we will gladly take that."

"Loud?" One of the other blue lanyard kids asked.

"Oh, I'm sorry. Weed," Malcom mocked.

"We are fresh out, dude. But you're in luck, bro," Conner said with excitement. "My cousin owns a dispensary not too far from here. We were on our way there to pick some stuff up. I can tell him to hook you up if you guys aren't scared."

"Let's do it," Malcom volunteered.

"I'm in," Scoop said.

"I'm out," Isaiah said.

I was the only one left. I didn't mind smoking again, but how were we going to get there was my only concern. There would be chaperones looking for us when they noticed we were gone. We would get suspended or even expelled if they found out we were going out on our own. Not to mention the drugs we were going to get. Then I would have to go to Tech, and that was not ideal for me. After the other three gave their answer, all of their eyes gazed upon me as if the fate of the world was my decision alone. I didn't want to go, but who would watch for Scoop? Malcom was a cool guy, but he didn't know how to handle him. Plus, there were five other guys we didn't even know who invited us, and I couldn't leave my friend like that. I finally mustered up enough thoughts to start talking.

"It's like five degrees outside with snow piled up to the moon. I don't know where this dispensary is, and we don't have a car that can fit eight people. And if we're walking, then I'm out too." Malcom and Scoop nodded in agreement. I guess I was the only one out of everybody, besides Isaiah, to think logically about the adventure they were so eager to take.

Conner leaned in and whispered, "I got you covered, bro. My cousin left his truck here in the parking lot with the keys in the glove compartment. Three can fit in the front, two can fit in the back, and the rest of us can ride on the flat bed."

"That's great and all, but while you guys figure out a way to not get caught, I'm going to take my food up to the room and chill before we have to go because you will not mess up my resume for college. Adios fellas, and good luck." Isaiah said while he chomped down on a bagel with butter spread on it. Three of Conners friends thought the same thing, said their goodbyes, and went to their room as well.

"Those guys were a bunch of losers anyways. They won't get a chance to take a hit off of anything we get either. My cousin Chad has every strand you can think of."

"We have to be back by 9:00 because we're not staying in Anchorage. We're leaving for Fairbanks at 10. In order for us, and I mean all three of us to go, we have to be back before 9:00."

I wanted to make sure that if I didn't go, then none of us would go. I didn't think that being that assertive would work, but I was in luck.

"All right, you got a deal. He's only about five miles down the road. It's ducked off in the woods but easy to find. Plus, we have iPhones, so I'll use the map to get us there and back. He's expecting us there now so let's get going."

"Hey," Tamar said, entering the breakfast area with Ashley A. "Where are you guys going?"

"Uh, we have to make a stop really quick," I answered. "You want to come with? We will be right back."

"Yeah, sure. Good thing we brought our jackets down," Tamar said.

"Uh dude, where are we going to sit? We're out, bro. We are not sitting in the bed of the truck, bro. Here take my cash and get me lemon haze." One of the remaining two of Conners friends said while they handed him the money and went back to their room.

"Come on guys don't be a douche. I don't even know these guys and you're going to leave me? Fine. Let's hurry up and go."

We rushed through the automatic doors of the lobby. The early Alaskan breeze smacked my face like a ton of bricks. My eyes immediately started to water due to thc brisk air. I was jealous of Tamar and Ashley A because they would at least be warm. It got cold in Wisconsin, but not this cold in March. We weaved through the parking lot to eventually see a pick-up truck that was lifted about six extra inches from its original build. It was a deep red Chevy with a matte black, block stripe going down the middle of the truck from the front to the back. The wheels were wrapped with the same matte black color. Conner slid into the driver's seat while I sat in the back between Ashley A and Tamar. Scoop and Malcom sat in the front. He started the truck and didn't even allow the car to warm up all the way before he pulled out of the hotel parking lot.

"Listen, I really don't think this is good idea. All of this for some weed? Y'all do know that if we get caught, we are going to get in more trouble than I think we would. Is getting high this worth it?" I asked.

"Well, I guess we're about to find out, aren't we?" Malcom replied. "For real though, we'll be gone twenty to thirty mins tops. Look," he pointed to Conner's GPS which was mounted on the dashboard, "It says we will get there at 8:45. His cousin is already there and is expecting him. I am sure Conner has to be back soon just like us because why would all of us hurry up and leave without any jackets on? Just relax, bro, we will be back in no time."

The unease I felt was nerve racking. I was unsure how Tamar felt about our adventure, but it seemed like she was cool with leaving and coming back. We were literally in a car with a stranger we had never met going to a weed dispensary in the middle of nowhere in the freezing cold of Alaska which was thousands of miles from Wisconsin. What made matters worse was it started snowing as soon as we turned the corner from the hotel. The ten-minute drive felt like a lifetime because the stakes were so high. The hotel we stayed at was outside the city near the woods. It was close to the road we had to take to get to Fairbanks. The dispensary was ten minutes further into the woods. We finally pulled into the front of the store and the parking lot was empty. It didn't look as special as I thought it would. We got out of the car and walked toward the front door. The hours of operation on the door said it opened at 10:00AM. Conner banged on the door, but no one answered. We had followed him thinking there would be someone there. All six of us were outside freezing and shivering.

"Isaiah?" Tamar asked in disbelief, "How did you get here?" Connor continued to knock at the door.

"I saw you going downstairs and heard that you were going with them. You know I have to make sure you stay out of trouble. Plus, dad would kill me if you got in trouble. I'm here to make sure you get back to the hotel."

"Bro, aren't you freezing with no jacket on?" Tamar asked.

"Yeah, I am, but I'll be fine since we will be leaving soon anyways."

"Look he's not here. Let's go because I am about to get frost bite out here," Scoop said, stuttering over his words.

"No man, he said he was going to be here. I'll call him really quick. As a matter of fact, let's go in the car to warm up," Conner replied.

We walked to the car and got back in our seats. There was not enough room for four people to be in the back seat, so we had to lap up. I was anxious because I thought Tamar was going to sit on my lap. She sat on her brother's lap instead.

"I am not getting any service at all. The call won't even go through. Any of you guys get any service?" Conner asked. We all looked at our phones and said no, one by one.

I spoke up and said, "I think this is a sign that we shouldn't have come."

Conner said, "I'm pissed. I have to get back anyways because we're flying back home today. Sorry for the blank trip guys. I'll text him I was here when I get service. He better believe I'm going to kick his ass at Thanksgiving for standing me up."

Conner tried to start up the truck, but it did not turn on. The engine kept turning and turning but it never did what it was supposed to do. There was an eerie nervousness throughout the vehicle. We were in the bitter cold of the Alaskan weather without jackets and heat. The snow started to fall harder, and you could hear the wind whistling on the surface of the truck. It seemed like the blizzard was on its way to us instead of missing us like they said. The sky was bright white as the clouds covered the sun. The spruce trees were brushed with white snow as the branches began to sway more violently. I had no clue where we were, and I couldn't come up with an idea on how to get back.

"Conner, do you know how to get back? Maybe we can walk back," Scoop proposed.

"Are you crazy dude? It's below freezing, and you want to walk five miles back to the hotel? I don't think so. Wait, I just remembered something. Chad has a greenhouse behind the store. Let's go back there to see if he's there."

We all got out of the car and quickly make our way behind the store. The green house was larger than the actual store. We trampled through the snow and found the door. Snow had gotten into my shoe and my socks got wet. Conner tried to open the door, but it was locked.

"You know what, screw this. I'm going to run to the car to get a jack and break the window of the store so we can go in. He can bill my dad because it's cold as balls out here." Conner ran to the car while we waited for his return.

"All this for some weed, huh?" I asked.

"Bro, chill out. We'll be fine. Y'all act like its hard drugs. Besides, who am I to pass up anything free?" Malcom replied.

"Yeah, but at what expense," Isaiah said. "We are outside freezing all because you wanted to get high."

"First of all, nobody asked your lame ass to come. You could have stayed in the hotel room."

"Yeah, I could have, but I need to make sure my sister was all right. What I look like letting my sister get in a car with a stranger and four guys? That's stupid."

"I really don't care, bro. If your sister and Ashley wasn't so thirsty, y'all wouldn't be here. Chill out before I really get mad."

"See Tamar, this is why I can't hang out with everybody. Its people like him that makes your life harder for no reason. He thinks he's big and bad because his dad played football. Nobody cares."

"What are you talking about? How is that even relevant right now? Nobody was even talking about my dad. And you better not say anything about him either. I'll beat your ass for real. The only reason I won't is because you've been cool up until this point. But don't play with me."

"Yo, yo, yo chill," I intervened. "Look, I know we are all irritated right now. It's cold, we are on edge because we are supposed to be at the hotel right now, and we are in the middle of nowhere. Let's focus on trying to get warm. At least the girls have jackets so they will be good. The argument that you guys are having is stupid. I'm shocked I am saying this to you, Isaiah. You are usually more levelheaded than me."

"Um," Scoop said concerned as soon as I finished my sentence. "Where did Conner and the truck go?"

We ran to the front of the dispensary to find nothing but tire tracks in the snow where the truck was. We were all puzzled. Conner had left us, and we had no way to get back to the hotel. The snow started coming down harder, and the wind started blowing faster. In that moment of disbelief, as snowflakes danced on my eyelashes, I had a quick thought of my mom. It was like

I was a toddler and she smiled at me while she wrapped me in a warm blanket. The cool Wisconsin winter had forced her to keep me warm in the house. I felt the warmth of her hug more than the blanket as she handed me over to a strange woman. I had never remembered that before. I was unsure if it was a daydream or an actual memory.

"So," Ashley A said with her hands in her pocket trying to stay warm, "What do we do now?"

Scoop looked up into the sky as a tree branch fell off a tree next to the store. "All I know is that it just got real."

CHAPTER NINE

You Can Trust Me

"Now that we are officially screwed, how are we going to get back?" Ashley A asked.

"I think we should walk back to the direction of the hotel. There were a few houses along the road." Malcom suggested.

Scoop agreed.

"I think we should bust this window open and stay in that dispensary and see if he has a phone." Isaiah said. "Why would we walk five miles in the snow where we have no clue where we are or where to go? Let's think people."

"I guess you're right," Malcom said, "But if I ever see that Conner dude again, I promise you I am beating him down. He got the truck started and left us. See, this is why you can't fully trust them white people."

Tamar responded, "There are plenty of great white people and plenty terrible black people so let's not play this game right now besides, this is not the place to have this conversation. So, who's going to break the window?"

All of us stood silent while the snow piled higher to where the snow was almost covering our shoes. I noticed a branch that fell beside the building. It wasn't a thin branch, but it was one that had girth to it. I thought that would be perfect to break the window. I didn't want anybody to use their fists because someone getting hurt would add more problems.

"Let's use that branch that fell."

"What?"

I yelled a little louder because the wind had picked up more.

"I said, let's use that branch over there to break the window."

I pointed to the branch and I noticed my index finger was shaking. The cold was already unbearable. The quicker we broke the window, the faster we could get to the warmth. Me, Malcom, Scoop, and Isaiah went to pick up the branch. It was almost fully submerged in snow, and we had to dig it out with our hands. We shoveled until we were able to lift it up from the ground. There was grass underneath where the branch was. Although it was dead, a few blades made an appearance.

"Let's bring it to the back and break one of those windows. Nobody would want to come to their business and have their front window broken. If we are going to do this, we can at least be courteous," Isaiah screamed.

Ashley A and Tamar followed us to the back. There were four windows spread out from one side of the building to the other. It looked like Scoop was the only one that would have been able to get through when we broke it. The window we zoned in on looked like the main office which had a direct line of sight to the green house. I could barely see inside because of the blowing snow from the ground and the trees. We readied ourselves to break the window until I heard a faint yelling behind me.

"Do you guys hear that behind us? It sounds like someone yelling."

"What?" The wind whistled and rushed past everyone's ears, and they couldn't hear me.

"I hear someone yelling. Can't you hear it?"

The boys looked behind themselves and yelled out no in unison. I gazed for a second longer as my nose ran and my eyes watered. I squinted and barely saw a small house with smoke coming out of the chimney in the distance behind the green house.

"Look," I hollered, "There's a house right there. I'm leaving." I let go of my end of the branch and ran towards the house. I didn't think about the rest of them, not even Tamar because I was so cold.

The house was further down because the dispensary was on top of a small hill. It felt like a long time for me to get to the house. It had to be about a mile jog. The hill helped me to run a little faster. My toes were frozen, and my hair was white. Not once did I look back and see where the others were.

Panting and out of breath, I pounded the door like I was trying to break it down. I looked back and saw the rest of them running at me. Someone came to the window and peered out of the curtains to see who it was. The door opened and standing there was a slender white guy with gray stringy hair with a bald spot and a beard like Santa Clause.

"What are you doing out here? Do you not know there's a snowicane hitting us now?" He had a deep Alaskan accent. Some people in Wisconsin and Minnesota sounded like him when they talked. They would sound really nasally and drag out the vowels. He motioned me inside of the house to some in. "Wait, are those y'er buddies coming too?"

"Yes." I whipped my hair back as the water splashed against the wooden walls.

"Well, they need to hurry it up because all the heat is escaping the house. What were you people doing out here anyways? That dispensary doesn't open until 10, but I don't think they will be open today. We got about twenty inches coming in."

The rest of the group came in the house and dusted themselves off from the snow. They were stomping and shaking their arms and heads. We looked distressed and defeated. We were lucky to find the house. I wanted to write because all of this would be great content for me.

"Why were you out here?" the man asked.

"Well, that is a long story," I said, "Could we use your phone? We have no service at all."

"You've came to the wrong house. I don't own a phone. Haven't for years."

"Would you be able to get us out of here back to the hotel? We are staying at the Condo Suites."

"Kid, I don't think you understood when I said twenty inches. Y'er on the edge of the bush right now my friend. Where y'er from?"

"We're from Wisconsin," Scoop said, while rubbing his arms to get warm.

"Here, come by the fire so you guys can get warm. I have so many questions for you. Let me go and fix you something. It's six of you so I'll bring out some hot chocolate."

He hobbled into the kitchen as if he needed a hip replacement. He prepared our drinks as we heard dishes clanging. We could hear a faint coughing coming from the kitchen. We sat down in the living room where the fireplace was. It felt so good to be warm. The house was a true cabin inside and out. He had a bear's head mounted right above the fireplace along with deer and other animals scattered above our heads. He had a case full of rifles, shotguns, and handguns. There was hardwood throughout, and you could hear every footstep. There was no upstairs but there was a door leading to what looked like a basement because there was a padlock on the door. My mind was racing to figure out what to do. I was unsure if I should trust this stranger or not. In reality, we had no choice because there was no other way.

"Yo, bro, you shouldn't give him so much information on us," Malcom whispered, "because we don't know who this dude is. He could end up being a serial killer or something. Who lives out in the middle of nowhere behind a dispensary?"

"What other choice do we have? You want to go back out in that cold to break into that place and potentially go to jail? You do know we are the only Black people in Alaska. There aren't many of us out here," I replied.

"Hey, I'm not Black," Ashley A responded.

"Man, we know that," Malcom said irritably. "We can look at you and tell. All I'm saying is that we need to be careful. I know that the teachers and them are looking for us right now trying to call us. What are we going to do if we have to stay the night here?”

Silence filled the room. We all knew what situation we were in, but we had not realized that we may be in real trouble. Six teenagers in a stranger's home is extremely odd. Thoughts and ideas filled the room with concerned looks and light groans. Our best bet was to stay here and wait until morning.

“I got something to keep ya warm,” the man said, carrying a tray-full of coffee cups with a bag marshmallows. “I don't have many visitors now-a-days. Darlene and I used to entertain years ago when we lived in the city until she got sick.” He grunted as he sat down on a dark wooden rocking chair with a colorful quilt laid on the back. “Stage IV cancer is a sumbitch. Thirty-eight years we were married. I loved that woman to life. The memory of her still lives in this house.”

His eyes teared up as he reminisced about Darlene. He kept talking and pulled out a handkerchief with the initials *D.O.O* stitched into it and caressed it on his cheek. The love he had for his wife was a beautiful sight to see. Creating a bond that lasts past death seemed beautiful. Although the gratefulness the man had for his wife was admirable, we still had to figure out how to stay safe in a stranger's home. I sipped from the steaming hot chocolate and it soothed my insides.

“Sir,” Isaiah asked while he drank, “What's your name and why did you move in the middle of nowhere?”

“It's been about seven years since I left the city. I've always loved the woods and being in nature. Off the grid is what you folks down in the lower Forty-eight call it. No electricity, no internet, just me and nature.”

Scoop asked, "What about your family? What if something happens to them how can they reach you?"

"I don't have any family left. Just me. My parents died when I was young, and I lived with my grandparents until I went to college. Been on my own ever since. I met Darlene in college, and we been inseparable ever since. Got married two weeks after we met. We didn't have kids. We lived a wonderful life, and I don't regret anything." He took a brief break to catch his breath.

"You know, death is always at your door, kids. You never know when your name is called. It's the never-ending cycle. Death called my parents, my grandparents, and my Darlene. My sweet Darlene. Ah! Why does death miss me! But I could go on and on about me. All I have is time. Why don't you tell me about you guys, and why you don't have any bunny boots?"

"School field trip," Tamar said. "We were with a friend at that store up there, but he left us after he finally got his car started."

"Let me guess, Northern Lights?"

"Yes."

"You can see them in Minnesota too. I understand why y'er school brought you all the way up here to see them. Aurora looks a little better. I'm a little biased because this is home f'er me."

"That's great," Malcom said with an attitude, "but to be honest, we really don't care about the Northern Lights right now. We are lost and can't get back to where we need to be. Are you sure there's no way we can get back to the road? There must be plow trucks salting the roads."

"Nope. Not until the snow stops. It's too dangerous out there. Even for them."

"Great. Thanks, uh, what's your name?" Malcom asked sarcastically

"If you want to know my name, just look over on that wall."

On the wall was a degree in engineering from the University of Alaska. His name was Raymond Oswald Oskee. I supposed he was a smart man. Underneath the degree was a certificate from BP for his outstanding work and research. We didn't care about that. As long as he wasn't weird, then we would be fine.

"I retired ten years ago," Raymond said, coughing violently into his handkerchief. "They said I only had a few months to go soon after retirement. I was able to outlive Darlene unfortunately." He coughed some more, and some blood spilled out into the handkerchief. "Excuse me for a minute while I get cleaned up."

He got up and went into the bathroom. The group looked at each other confused and concerned.

"Ok, is it me or does this guy seem creepy?" Ashley A asked.

"Uh, yea, really weird. He keeps talking about his wife and dying. All we did was ask about his name," Tamar answered.

"Ok, so we need to figure out a plan here," Isaiah proposed. "We have to figure out what are we going to do. What if this storm lasts days instead of just today? How are we going to get back or contact anybody?

Silence.

"All right, thanks for the help, guys. After the blizzard passes, we should go back to the dispensary and call for help. Until then we stick together and make sure this guy doesn't try anything funny. It is still early and it's a good thing we ate a little something, so we don't have to bother Ray for any food."

"Speak for yourself. Ashley and I didn't eat. We had just come down from our room to grab food before we left. I'm kind of hungry."

"Ok, does anyone have snacks?" Isaiah asked.

The wind picked up speed.

"This isn't going to work if everybody is silent. We have to communicate."

I loved the way Isaiah took charge and stayed calm. I felt a responsibility to lean toward being a leader like him.

"I got nothing."

"Me too."

"I got a couple gummies left," Malcom said with a grin on his face.

"Is that all you do is get high?" Isaiah asked.

"Man, I'm high all the time. Even when I'm on the field. I'm just built different."

Isaiah shook his head in condemnation.

I decided to make a suggestion. "Let's check our phone to see if we have service. Maybe there is a spot where we can get signal."

Everyone got up and started walking around with their phones in their hands as if we were searching for treasure in sand dunes. After a few minutes of walking, we all met back by the fireplace. Once again, there was silence as we plopped down in our seats. The wind beat against the cabin while the snow billowed, rising slowly inch by inch.

"So now what?" Scoop asked with anxiety.

"We wait it out."

"I think J is right," Isaiah agreed. "Let's wait it out and see if Ray can bring us back to civilization. Besides, have you guys seen Ray? It's been a while."

We shrugged our shoulders and looked around the room.

"While you guys figure that out, I'll go to the bathroom," Ashley A said.

She stumbled around the cabin trying to find the bathroom. All of a sudden, there was a loud thud, and a tooth shattering shriek filled the cabin. We jumped from our seats and followed the scream.

Raymond lay in the bathroom lifeless as blood from his mouth spilled onto the floor mat. He held on to the handkerchief with Darlene's initials under his cheek. I saw this picture with B before I left the house. I felt uneasy at that moment, but Malcom broke me out of the trance.

"Yo, is he for real dead? I've never seen a dead body before."

"Oh my god, oh my god, oh my god. What are we going to do now? We're alone," Ashley A said, crying.

Everybody talked and panicked at the same time. I was the only person calm.

"All right guys, let's not panic." I made my best Isaiah impression to sound more like myself. "We should get the door open over there with that lock on it. Maybe that leads to a basement. We can put him down there until the storm is over. We can call the police after we get some help."

"I cannot go to jail. My parents will flip out on me. A dead guy? We shouldn't call the police. Besides, we were going to buy marijuana at a dispensary underage."

"Wait, what? I think you're thinking too much into it, Ashley. Just calm down," Tamar said.

"I'm not freaking out. I'm just being realistic. My dad is a lawyer and I hear about cases like this all the time. It's going to get pinned on someone. TLC you're good because you're a woman. One of you is going to get charged with something. Everybody is a suspect. And yes, even you Isaiah will be looked at as a criminal."

Scoop rolled his eyes and started walking toward the locked door, punching his fist into his hand.

"See, this is why my dad always told me to never mess with them too many people because when sticky situations come, the ones you don't really know won't be there for you."

"All right, so I guess I'll be the voice of reason," Isaiah interjected. "Ashley, I think you're just nervous like all of us. This is the first dead body we've seen, but we have to be calm."

Not my first time I saw a dead body.

"Let's get this door open and put him down there and then we can figure things out..." Isaiah paused. "We didn't even check to see if he was really dead. We have to check his pulse."

We looked at each other to see who was going to volunteer first. Tamar puffed out air and jarred out, "I'll do it," and stormed over to where Ray was slumped.

She bent down and looked at him, gagging and coughing. Ray was on his side with his arm underneath him. His head was slightly tilted to the ground, so Tamar had to rotate his head to check his pulse in his neck. She placed her finger in his neck slowly and waited to see if she felt anything. After twenty seconds of searching and holding, she looked up at us and shook her head no.

"So now that we know he's dead, let's find something to get that padlock off of the hinge," Malcom said and he immediately raged the kitchen counters, cabinets, and drawers to find something. The rest of us joined in looking in other rooms. I stopped to look at what kind of screwdriver was needed to take the whole door down off the hinges. I needed a flat head screwdriver.

"Found a set a keys!" Tamar yelled.

We ran to the door to claim our prize. There had to be twenty-five keys on that set, but we were determined to try every single one. One after another we tried and failed. We may have even used the same key twice on accident.

Finally, as the keys fumbled through Tamar's hands, we found a key that unlocked Ray's temporary grave. The door creaked opened as the light faded the deeper you looked down the stairs. It was dark and you couldn't see past the sixth step. The stench of moth balls rose through the atmosphere to the top step. The boys and I assumed our positions to pick up Ray's body and dispose of him in the basement. He was much lighter than that branch we had earlier. Scoop and I had the legs while Malcom and Isaiah had his arms.

We stumbled down the stairs while the girls followed behind us. There was a hush among us while we carried Ray. The wind wasn't whittling anymore, at this point it was monstrous gusts that shook the cabin. There were fishing poles, nets, boots, a blanket, and other outdoor gear in every corner of the basement. We found a large tarp that covered what looked like a medical cart, but we paid those things no mine because we needed to get Ray wrapped up. Scoop took the items that were on top of the tarp and dumped them on the cold concrete. We spread out the tarp as wide as it went and rolled the body. By the time we were done, it looked like a poorly made pig in a blanket. His legs were showing from his knees down while his stringy hair peeked through the top.

"Well, any last words?" Isaiah asked.

"Really, we are not doing this. I'm going upstairs. It is freezing." Tamar darted up the stairs while they followed one by one.

I was the last one to go upstairs. I stared at the body while the howling continued. Regret overpowered me. I didn't know who Ray was, but it sounded like he'd loved his wife. That's all he talked about the short time we had with him. I never imagined loving someone that hard, and then one day they disappear. The only one that I could love was my mom, but I had no memory of her. I walked up the stairs to meet the group by the fireplace.

Wails of wind filled the cabin. The once discreet, quaint home turned into a sanctuary for all six of us. We were safe from the weather but not our situation. We were all lost in a place that no one was familiar with. Our nerves were high. We didn't know how long we would be in this situation. The only thing we had was ourselves. No parents, chaperones, or phones. Just us and nature.

"Now that we know that Ray is dead, we have to find food. I'll go in the kitchen to see if there's anything. We need a volunteer to go back downstairs and see if there is something there too. We know we have running water and heat. At least for now," Isaiah said.

"I'll come with you. If I find something I like, I'm claiming to it first, so I don't want to hear any complaints," Scoop said.

"I'll check in the basement. Ashley, you want to come with me?" Malcom inquired devilishly.

"Ewe, with the dead guy? I think not. I'll go with Isaiah, and Scoop can go with you."

Isaiah said agitated, "Look I don't care who goes with who we have to find some food. Come with me Ashley and Scoop go with Malcom. J, you, and Tamar can try and find some more wood or anything to keep the fire going."

Everybody went to their areas to search. Tamar and I walked to the next room over and searched for firewood. That was my moment to start a meaningful conversation with her. Emotions were high and we were all vulnerable. I thought maybe she would open up.

"Man, this is crazy right? What are the odds of this happening? They said that the storm was going to pass over us, but it seems like it hit us really good, huh?" I said starting a conversation.

"Yeah." Tamar said uninterested while looking through a box full of papers.

"You think it'll all be over soon?"

"I hope so."

I didn't know what I did to get those short responses, so I decided to ask.

"Did I do something to you? You seem like you don't want to talk to me?"

"I'm sorry. I'm just so nervous. There's a dead guy underneath us, and we're trapped in a cabin in a snowstorm. I didn't plan on this happening, so I'm just trying to gather my thoughts and everything."

Tamar pushed the box away from her as she was squatted, and she sat down in the middle of the floor. The room we were in was where Ray stored all his documents and mementos of his family. There were no desks, chairs, or any furniture. There was only a closet, boxes stacked almost to the ceiling, a window that was covered in snow, and pictures of everyone he knew. I stopped searching in the closet and sat next to Tamar.

"Well, if this means anything, I'm not that nervous. I'm used to being in situations like this."

"You've been in a snowstorm with a dead guy?"

"No. Not exactly that. I'm used to being uncomfortable."

"It's your dad, huh? Parents can be too much at times. I know my parents are. They put so much pressure on us to be role models and be great. It seems like I can't be a teenager sometimes. You know? Look at me, I did it again. I guess my biggest flaw is assuming I know people and their problems. Why are you comfortable being uncomfortable?"

I hesitated to open up. I wanted for her to talk about herself some more, but it seemed like it was a moment for me to open up. She felt safe. It felt like I could be myself around her. Her personality was like Isaiah's. It was something about them that made me want to just talk. With Isaiah, I held back, but with Tamar I didn't.

"Well, I'm not in a situation like yours. I live with my foster mom and she isn't easy to live with. She hates me. I feel like the only reason why she has me is because she gets paid from the state. My dad has been in jail since I was little. I don't know what happened. I used to write him, but the letters stopped coming after a while. The only reason I know what he looks like is because I have an old picture of him and my mom. There were times where I felt like I couldn't breathe. B is such a bad person. I remember one time when I was eleven, I fell asleep with the tv on in the living room one night, and she was pissed. In the middle of the night, she woke me up and forced me to write *I am a stupid Black kid* 100 times. Another time she told me the only thing that I am good for is being dead beat and a criminal. She would mentally and verbally taunt me on a daily basis. Sometimes I wished she would have just beaten me and got it over with. I can deal with physical scars."

Tamar started crying. I held my tears in.

"You know, I've lived with that woman for five years of my life, and she has never smiled at me once. The only time I got a break from her is when she was passed out drunk. A few months ago, she had an accident and fell down the stairs because I finally got the balls to cuss her out. That was the last time I heard her say anything to me. I called 911 because I was scared. I've been taking care of her since December. Think about how crazy life is. I have to feed her and bathe her. Most people my age would have left her to dry, but since she's been in a wheelchair, the house has been clean, I have groceries at home because I go to the store and buy actual food instead of beer and cigarettes, and I have some peace. I usually write in my notebook about what goes on in my life. Most of the time is poetry. I know it seems soft, but writing has been my thing since I can remember. It keeps me from hurting myself. I usually don't talk to people like this because I was so beaten down by B that I was afraid. This may sound funny but when you hit me in gym class, that was like a wakeup call for me. I had felt like I had never been in control of anything in my life until then. I vowed that I will be in control from that point on. That's why I'm telling you all of this. I want to be in control of my own story. So, when I say that being uncomfortable is normal for me, it's not a once in a while thing. It has been my whole life."

Tamar stood up and grabbed a box of tissue to wipe her eyes. She gave me a couple sheets, and I wiped my tears that I couldn't hold in any longer. My emotions busted out of me because I had to look back and deal with my pain out loud and direct instead of artistically on paper.

"Being judged based on my hair, my skin color, and where I live is hard enough with going to the store and school. On top of that, when I come home, I have no family. The closest thing to family I have is Scoop. He's been around since I was eleven, and I almost lost him to a stupid argument. Even sometimes with him it's exhausting because he gets so emotional with the smallest things. I tried to be strong and make it seem like I wasn't bothered, but I was. One day I dreamt of killing myself. There was a point where I didn't know if I was dreaming or not, and I wanted to let go of everything. I see people like you and your brother, Malcolm, everybody at school, and even Scoop who have both parents and money isn't a concern. I'm only at South Shore because of a lottery. I know it's not your fault and everybody has their own paths, but I would kill to have it like you guys. I know it sounds like I'm all over the place, but I've never opened up to anyone.

"I imagine waking up to love every day. I imagine having a future that's clear no matter where I go or what I do. Even now when this is all over, your parents will be concerned about your well-being. Did you get hurt? Or are you ok? When I get home…well, I don't know if B will even be alive. You know what, I'm sorry." I wiped my eyes dry and stood up. "You probably think I'm weak because I'm crying and a lame because of what I told you. Let's just go and find some firewood."

Tamar stood up and held her hand out for me to stand up with her. She looked at me in the eyes with empathy.

"You listen, I have my struggles, yes, but I know that there are people like you who kill to be in my position. I take for granted where I'm at while there are strong people like you who have to suffer so much and make life look easy while I complain about the smallest thing. Two things my dad always tell me is pain brings character. You wouldn't be at the school if your character wasn't high. You matter and I don't care what anyone says, you're not dumb, stupid, or worthless. The second thing is Black men need to open up more and be vulnerable. You are expected to take so much pain and hide it under the pride of a man. You mean something to so many people, and you don't even know it. You just helped me put my life into perspective by telling your story. You have always been in control of your story. It just took you a while to realize it. Don't hide that."

Tamar leaned in and embraced me. I felt love for the first time. Her arms wrapped over my shoulders and her head leaned next to my neck. I heard her sniffle. Her hair was tickling the back of my neck while she stood on her tippy toes because I was a taller than her. Her hug felt like hope when all hope was lost. If I hadn't been in love, I was now. Tamar's embrace was everything I imagined.

We pulled our heads back and looked at each other with teary eyes. The connection was there, and it seemed inevitable that we would kiss. I was nervous. Not because of the story I told her, but because of the emotion I felt that I've never felt before. The puppy love started from my feet and ended at the crown of my head. Butterflies tingled my stomach as our lips came closer to connecting. I made the final push and we kissed. It wasn't a peck, but it was a sensual kiss that I wanted to last forever. We pulled back and hugged again even longer.

"Tamar, I like you, but please don't tell anybody about B. I don't know if she was alive before I left. I feel bad because she was in the bathroom dying out before we got here. I don't know what to do."

"James, listen to me. I got you. We can figure this all out after we get into a safe place. And don't worry, you can trust me. Besides, I like you too." She winked at me and kissed me again. "Come on, let's find this firewood."

The butterflies stayed in my stomach.

We walked around in all the other rooms and couldn't find firewood anywhere. After our failed mission, we sat down in the living room defeated.

"If push comes to shove, we can use those papers and junk in Ray's room to keep us warm." I suggested. "Wait a minute, maybe there is some chopped wood outside next to the cabin."

"Why would there be any there?" Tamar asked.

"I don't know. It seems like something Ray would do, I guess. And they have stuff like that in movies. It wouldn't hurt to check. I know it's too small, but could I use your jacket to go outside? At least I can stay a little warm trying to find the wood."

Tamar took off her jacket and handed it to me. When I put it on, I could smell her perfume that was on her shirt in the inside of the jacket. It was a soft smell that made me smile. I could tell it wasn't cheap spray from a strip mall, but it was a sophisticated fragrance that left an impression. I walked toward the door and put my shoes on. My socks were damp because of the puddle that our shoes had left from the snow earlier. The jacket had just barely reached the middle of my forearm. I couldn't zip it up because I was afraid it would rip. I put my hand on the door-knob and Tamar gently tapped my shoulder and I turned my head toward her.

"Be careful."

I nodded and opened the door. The wind almost knocked us over. The gusts blew snow into my eyes and the snow that was piled up on the door had fallen into the doorway. I had to take long steps to make a path to get outside. Eventually, I closed the door behind me and started walking along the side of the cabin. The snow was up to my knee, and it was hard to navigate. If I made the wrong move, it could have been trouble for me. I had never seen outside so white before even though my eyes were hardly open.

I made it to the back of the cabin, and I saw what looked like a metal bar sticking out of the back. It was a latch that was attached to a cellar door. I guessed Ray had the bar high enough for bad snowstorms. I struggled to turn the latch, but eventually I got it open. There was a ramp that led down to a small room filled with chopped wood. It was a door on the wall of the room, but it was locked. It looked like it led to the basement. I grabbed as much wood as I could so we could keep the fire going. I stumbled along the path I had originally made to get back inside the cabin. I stomped inside the doorway as I felt the snow mush against my feet. I went into the living room where the fire was and set the wood in front of the fireplace. By this time, everyone had finished their search and was sitting down.

"Look at my guy come through. Good stuff lumberjack J." Scoop said.

"Man, it's so much wood down there already chopped. At least we won't have to worry about getting cold anytime soon," I replied.

"Good," Isaiah said, "at least you got good news. I only found a couple of cans of baked beans and corn in the kitchen. Malcom and Scoop didn't find anything. Ashley had found a box of spaghetti but that's it. We have to make this last until we can get back to the group. Was that all the firewood you found?"

"No," I said while shaking my shoes out, "there is still more in the room from outside. We should hurry up and get all of it because it seems like the windows and doors will be covered in snow before it stops snowing."

The guys put their shoes back on and took a few trips with me to get most of the wood from behind the cabin. The snow was rising faster and faster with every trip. When we were finished, we looked like walking snowmen. A large pile of wood was in the middle of the floor waiting to be burned. Ray had a fireplace kit next to the entrance of the room right next to the chair he sat in. We gathered scrap paper from the room Tamar and I had my first intimate encounter. The fire was blazing well, so we didn't do anything to it.

We sat in silence for what seemed like a lifetime. Tamar sat next to me on the love seat while everyone else had their own separate seats. The energy in the room seemed lost and confused. Surprisingly, Isaiah didn't have a speech or anything positive to say. I pulled out my phone and started to write since I didn't have my notebook with me.

Shades of Love March 16th, 12:32PM

Love isn't a color it's more like light. It turns your cold heart warm and your dark days bright. Love isn't love until it's cultivated. You must plant the seed of like and water the soil of emotions until it's saturated. Love doesn't hurt when you feel it in your bones. It soothes and smooths like delicate musical tones. Love is packaged in thoughts and actions. Its more than 'I Love You,' it's more than reactions. How was love created? Can only one person have it? Can love be felt? Can you literally grab it? Everybody wants it, and some rarely experience it. A few actually found love, but only when they've dreamt it.

"What are you writing?" Tamar whispered as she looked over at my phone while I was typing.

"Oh, nothing. Just something stupid," I said, embarrassed.

"Let me see it."

I didn't want her to read what I had wrote because I didn't want her to think I was catching feelings too soon. We had just kissed, and we didn't even go that far yet. I was afraid that she would laugh at my work. I wanted to be that tough guy for her, but I was too emotional to portray that type of character. It wasn't me.

"I don't think you'll like it," I said.

"Well, you will never know until I see."

I handed her my phone and she read the poem. As she was reading it, she placed her left hand on her heart, then over her mouth. I didn't know if that was a good sign or not. I couldn't read her, but clearly, she read me. I'd never let anyone read my stuff. Not even Scoop. Reading my poem, she held my entire makeup in her hand.

"James. You don't know how good that is. It's beautiful." Tamar said with a smile.

"Tamar, you got my guy writing love songs to you?" Malcom said, lying back in his seat laughing. I didn't know he could hear us talking over the wind.

"Come on bro. It's nothing like that."

"Come on now. Why can't guys be romantic?" Tamar asked.

"Romantic? My nigga is soft. Romance has nothing to do with being all mushy. It's about spending bread and showing a woman a good time. Once in a while you can throw in some smooth words, but other than that women now-a-days love real niggas."

Tamar groaned. I felt I had to defend the honor of my un-official girlfriend, so I chimed in.

"I can explain what I wrote. I am a writer and I love to write. Sometimes I write about real things that happen in life, and sometimes I write about fantasies, and sometimes I write about my life. It just so happened, Tamar wanted to see what I wrote, and she liked it. If you want, I can be a ghost writer for you if you want to be a rapper." Everyone laughed at what I said except Malcom.

"Lover boy got jokes. All I'm saying is this, girls want the mysterious bad boy. They don't want no soft wannabe poet. Look at all the baddest chicks right now. They all want that tough guy." Malcom explained while he stood up and leaned against the fireplace.

"No. That's not it. Most girls I know don't like guys like that at all. Meaning guys like you, Malcom," Tamar included.

"What do you mean guys like me?"

"Guys that think that they are all of that because they have money."

"Check." Malcom gestured with his fingers a check mark.

"Guys that think they look sooo good."

"Check."

"Guys that think they have a chance with every girl because they have a small penis."

"Che—" Malcolm stopped before he could finish. Everyone laughed again.

"Yeah. Don't come for us girls. We're not idiots." Tamar was good enough to where she didn't need my help at all. "Besides, if I want to date somebody like J, I can and will."

Everyone looked at each other in shock because what Tamar had said came out of nowhere.

"Uh, is anybody hungry? I sure can go for some beans and corn." Scoop said rubbing his stomach in an obvious mocking voice to switch the mood.

"Yeah, we should start getting some food in us. It's getting late," Isaiah said. "We have to ration the food because we don't know how long we might be here."

Isaiah went to the kitchen and Ashley A followed him and started making dinner.

"I'm good on them beans, bro." Malcom suggested, "I got these gummies. Being in here with y'all niggas, imma need to be high anyways.

"I need some of them too. Malcom. Throw some my way." Scoop said while he cupped his hands.

"I'm tired, so I'm going to lie down," I shouted to Isaiah.

I got up and went to Ray's room and grabbed a blanket from the closet. Tamar followed me in the room we kissed in and we both fell asleep on the floor.

CHAPTER TEN

Time To Go

"*Right!*" *The gun was pointed directly in the middle of my eyes. The rage the gunman had was enough to murder me. I got down on my knees with my hands behind my head.*

"*Who are you?*" *The man shouted with an all-black hoodie on with a police badge pinned to him. I couldn't make out his face.*

"*I said right!*" *I didn't understand what he wanted. I lifted my right hand in the air.*

"*Boy I said write!*" *B's voice pelted out of nowhere, and I stood up to see where her voice came from. I ran and, immediately, I was on the track again racing. The crowd was throwing things at me, but this time I ran fast enough to dodge them. I saw the finish line just ahead was Tamar and my mom holding whom I figured was me when I was a baby. It was the same vision I had right before we got out of the snow. Just before I crossed the finish line, I looked to my right, and the hooded man had the gun pointed at my face while he ran. All of a sudden—*

Pow! I jumped up in the middle of the night out of my sleep shaking because of the dream. It seemed like my life was trying to tell me something in my dreams. I woke up in a cold sweat shivering because the temperature dropped in the house. Tamar was lying next to me sound asleep. I gently stood up and tip-toed into the living room where the rest of the guys were asleep. The fire was almost out so I grabbed the papers and wood and put them in the fireplace with the small flames. After a few minutes, the fire got bigger, and it had gotten warmer. The left side of my body was aching because I was sleeping on the wood. I knew if I was in pain, Tamar would too. I went back into the room and woke her up as quiet as I could. You could hear the floor creak with every step.

I whispered, "Hey. Tamar." She was so beautiful even when she slept. "Tamar. Wake up. Go into the bedroom and lie on the bed. I know the floor is uncomfortable."

Tamar got up and went to the bathroom, then went into the bedroom. Before she lay down, she motioned me to go with her. I quietly declined. She loudly whispered, "come on." I obliged her request. I crawled into the bed with her and cuddled underneath the covers. I didn't know how to position myself in the bed with her because I had never done it before. I knew I was awkward and fidgety, so I made myself lie still with some space between myself and Tamar because I didn't want her to get me too excited. She shimmied closer to me and grabbed my arm to wrap around her as she faced the wall.

The bed was uncomfortable because I felt the spring underneath the padding. Anything was better than the floor at that point. The wind never lost its intensity as the night grew. I checked my phone to see what time it was, but it was dead. My mind started to go in a million places at once. It raced from my dream to B lying on the floor to Tamar to getting in trouble, back to B, my mom, my dad to Tamar. My thoughts were everywhere, and I couldn't go back to sleep. It seemed like the storm wouldn't let up just like my life. I had two options: to either make the best out of a bad situation or give up like I used to do and allow whatever to happen and fall back into that same old tired James. Yet, I was too determined to stand firm.

Tamar moved a little closer.

I tried to decipher what my dreams meant. I couldn't shake it. I moved to the edge of the bed and sat up with my feet on the cool floor. Tamar turned around facing me while she hugged the pillow.

"You ok?"

"Oh. Yeah. I'm good. I just had a weird dream that's all."

"Tell me about it. I don't think I'll be able to go to sleep soon anyways."

The bed squeaked as I inched toward her. She sat cross-legged and yawned while she hugged the pillow.

"Well, I had this dream when I was on the plane where I was running in the Olympics or something. When I was running, the crowd started throwing garbage at me. I fell because I was trying to dodge the stuff they were throwing. As I got closer to the finish line, I started floating and then I woke up. Then just before I got up a few minutes ago, there was this guy with a hoodie and a police badge holding a gun to my head yelling at me. I don't know if he was saying 'right' in terms of the direction or 'write' in terms of like pen and paper. But then, the voice sounded like B and then I went to the same track I was in as my last dream. Same thing happened like before, but I saw you and my mom at the finish line. Then, right before I crossed, I looked to the right and the guy in the hoodie shot me, and then I woke up. I know that was a weird dream, but I don't know if it meant something or not."

"I think you're stressed out about a lot of the things people are trying to throw at you. I know life can be rough, but I look at life as a race and I think your mind is doing the same thing. The guy with the gun could be the police officer you and Scoop had that encounter with. Your mind is telling you to keep on writing because you're doing the right thing with your talent. It just takes an authority figure for you to actually realize how great of a writer you are because you're almost at the finish line. As for me and your mom, maybe I remind you of your mom or something."

"How do you and your brother do that?"

"Do what?" Tamar inquired.

"You both know how to read me and my situation."

"Well, when you say 'read me', you make it seem like we're psychics or something." Tamar chuckled then let out a nervous sigh. "Well, I have this thing where I'm interested in dreams. I think dreams have hidden meanings, and they can be deciphered. I can understand dreams, and Isaiah can understand people. It's like a gift."

"That's funny because he said the same thing. He's a psychic. I knew it."

"No, we call it a prophet in the Bible."

"What's the difference?" I asked.

Tamar chuckled again with a sigh of delight.

"How much time do you have? To give you a short answer, the difference is who you serve as God. If you serve Jesus, then you a prophet, and if you serve anyone or anything else, you're a psychic."

I decided to test her on her religion. I figured since we're up, I could measure up to see if she was as sharp as Isaiah.

"So, I can be a prophet if I serve Jesus then?"

"It's not that simple. Your gift is writing. There was a King named David and he wrote songs and poems, and he is considered a type of prophet because he referenced Jesus on multiple occasions. I don't know what God has for you, but you may have the same gifts as he had. Let me pray for you so God can show you."

My plan backfired. I was not ready to be prayed for. I didn't know how to pray or what to pray for. I wasn't the religious type, but this didn't seem like religion. It felt like something else. Tamar grabbed my hand and let out a big yawn before she grabbed my other hand. Her hands were so smooth. I didn't want to pray, but I didn't want to let go of her hands. She bowed her head down, closed her eyes, and cleared her throat. She felt me staring, and she opened her left eye sightly and said with a smile, "Close your eyes." I obliged.

"Father God, we thank you for your grace and mercy you have shown us. We thank you for a place to sleep tonight and food. We are not where we want to be, but we are where we should be. Lord, I pray that you show James who you are and what you want him to be. Show yourself mighty in his life and let his eyes be opened to the truth. Reveal yourself to him in his dreams, his life, and his writings. Let the gift that you have given him become evidence of your love. I pray that you keep us safe while we're here and keep us protected in Jesus' name I pray. Amen."

"So that's it?"

"Yep. I'm sleepy so I'm going to go back to bed. You should try too. We might have another long day tomorrow."

After she prayed, I didn't feel any different. The only thing that changed was my hands was sweaty and I was a little excited. I figured nothing else would happen, so I lay down and closed my eyes and went back to sleep.

The next morning, I woke up and Tamar wasn't in the room with me. I sat up with my feet on the bed and stretched. My morning breath was always horrible. I looked in the room to find toothpaste. I had no luck. I decided to go into the bathroom to rinse out my mouth before I started talking to anyone. After I finished, I went into the living room where everyone was talking. When I entered the room, they all became silent as if I was a stranger.

"Did I interrupt something?" I asked.

"Finally, dude. You been sleep for a minute." Scoop said. "We been up for at least three hours."

"What time is it?"

Scoop pulled his phone out of his pocket, "12:15."

I didn't know I had slept that late. It must have been from the stress of the day before.

"Now that sleeping beauty is up, what is the plan?" Malcom asked everybody.

"After we make some food, I think we should look for a phone or another person. We need to let people know where we are," Ashley A suggested.

"I don't think it's a good idea that we leave the house," Isaiah said. "We have food here, enough firewood to keep the fire going, and shelter."

"Don't forget the dead nigga in the basement." Scoop acknowledged.

"Oh right, I forgot, we have a murder case on our hands too. How could I forget that?" Ashley A said.

Eruption broke out. Everyone was talking over one another. It was like an episode of *Love and Hip Hop*. There were curse words flying everywhere. Mainly from Malcom and Ashley. It was so loud that I could barely think. I went back into Ray's bedroom to think. Everyone was stressed out and nervous. Five teenagers stuck in the middle of nowhere with nowhere to go because of an act of God. No phones, just humans. The only thing they could do was fight.

I paced back and forth and tried to devise a plan that could get us to safety. We could go back to the dispensary and break the window open and hope that there was a phone. If we did that, we would have to walk up the hill with the snow to our waists. There was nothing else around us that could get us from where we were. We were stuck. The only other option was to wait a few days and then go back up the hill. I wasn't sure that everyone else would like that idea except for Isaiah. As I thought, the floor creaked with every step.

I noticed a window in the room that was covered with snow. I opened it and cleared it off so I could see through it. As I looked out of the opened window, I saw in the distance a bridge with what looked like a snowplow smashing through the snow. I couldn't see clearly because of the blowing snow. I went back into the living room where everyone was arguing, and I was able to pull Scoop aside without anyone noticing. I brought him into the room and told him to look out of the window and tell me what he saw.

"Well, it's hard to see because of the blowing snow, but it looks like a bridge. And I think that's a truck up there."

"You think we can make it?" I asked.

"By walking?"

"Yeah."

"Hell naw!" Scoop exclaimed. "Bro, we don't know if there's ice down there under the bridge, we don't know it there is a ladder to get on the bridge, and the snow would be up to our thighs. You're tripping, bro."

"I'm not staying here man. It's time to go. We are going to kill each other here." I pleaded my case as best as I could.

We were quiet for a second until a thought came into my head.

"What if we used the cart that was in the basement? I think we could use that."

"With like a foot or two of snow? Yeah, you're crazy."

"Let's just see."

Scoop reluctantly agreed and we hustled to put our shoes on and ran down in the basement where Ray was. We found the cart that the tarp was on we wrapped Ray in. Lucky for us, it had a plow on the front. We thought we'd reached the jackpot. Our emotions overcame us, and we lifted up a shout of excitement. We darted upstairs and interrupted the argument.

"We found a snowplow," I explained. "It's small, but I think that we should try and make a path back to this bridge me and Scoop saw. There was a snow truck that was plowing the street not too far ahead."

The room became quiet with everyone thinking. The snow had stopped, but the wind was still relentless. The windows started to shake, and branches were flying everywhere. The worst of the storm was over, but it was the lingering effects that made everything still feel like a storm was going on. I plopped down on the couch to catch my breath from running up the stairs from the basement to explain my potential plan.

"I don't think we should go anywhere. We're warm, we have a little bit of food, and we're safe. Let's chill for a little longer." Isaiah gave his appeal.

"Naw, let's bounce. I don't know how much longer I can stay in this house with Ashley. She's crazy," Malcom said.

"As much as I would love to leave and get away from this creep, Isaiah's right. We should stay even though we're going to be doing twenty-five to life." Ashley said with a condescending tone while fixing her hair.

"Ashley!" Scoop yelled, "You gotta relax. Nobody is going to jail. We're just trying to find out a way to get out of here. But I do agree that we should stay."

Tamar raised her hand timidly as if she was in class and suggested, "How about this, J, Scoop, and Malcom go and the rest of us can stay until you bring back some help. Going with only two people would be bad."

"I'm good on that," Scoop said nervously, scratching his arm, "Isaiah can go."

"Nope. I have to stay with my sister. I would love to come out there in the cold and help, but I'm not going out like that."

Isaiah was keen to the fact that family was a priority. His dad developed that trait in him. Although Tamar was older, he always looked out for her like she was the youngest. Seeing this built up a greater respect I had for him. I admired Isaiah for following the beat of his own drum.

"Ok fine, I won't let my guy go out like that. I got you J. Let's get that plow going so we can get up out of here," Scoop said as he lifted his sleeves as if he was strong. I could always count on Scoop to have my back even though he wanted to stay.

We went to the basement and strategized on how to get the snowplow through the cellar the easiest way possible. Luckily enough, there was a doorknob on the inside of the room of the cellar from the basement. We lifted and turned the plow every which way to make it fit. The doorway was wide enough, but the plow was heavy because of the giant hunk of metal on the front. We didn't want to get cut by it either, so we were being cautious. We took a few minutes to catch our breath since we exerted a lot of energy. We had our hands on our knees and above our heads as if we had just ran sprints.

"Look!" Scoop yelled out. "There's a rope. How about two of us pull it up the stairs and the other person can stand behind it and make sure that it does not catch on the steps."

Malcom and I were bigger than Scoop, so we volunteered to pull while Scoop guided it.

I decided to lead the charge.

"After I open the door, I'll count from three and that's when you guide it, Scoop. Me and Malcom are going to try and get this thing up here as quick as possible." I walked up the stairs to open the door while Malcom tied the rope to the steering wheel. We all got into position to make our escape.

The wind had died completely. The once fearful wind had subsided quickly, but I was unsure for how long. I looked outside and I only saw the top of the snow-covered trees that looked like cauliflower. I hadn't smelled the air until now. I could taste freedom through my nose. The crisp air tickled the hair on the back of my neck. There was a break in the clouds where the sun gently snuck its rays through to the snow. The glistening white flakes on the ground reflected the gleams of the sun back to the sky. There was snow on the top two stairs as if it was welcoming us to civilization.

We pulled and Scoop pushed. We pulled again and Scoop pushed. We pulled and pulled, until the plow was outside of the cabin. We all beat our chests and boasted while the sun was in full shine. I got snow in my shoes, but I didn't care. We were that much closer to safety. We flipped the plow right side up and sat down on it. As we were getting ready to leave, there was one problem.

"Does anyone have the keys?" I asked, leaning back in the driver side.

The only answer was the easy wind blowing passed my ears. The wind started to blow again.

"I'll see if Tamar still has those keys from yesterday. One of then should work."

Scoop sprinted downstairs to get the keys from Tamar. Malcom sat back and ate another gummy. He kicked back and sat as if he had no care in the world. I'd never spent any length of time with him at all by myself, so I decided to ask him a question.

"Hey, I know you probably don't like talking about this, but where is your mom? We know about your dad, but you never mention your mom. If you don't want to talk about it then it's cool. I understand."

I didn't want to sit in silence, and I wanted to know a little bit more about him than football and money.

Malcom took a deep sigh and said mumbled under his breath,

"Thank God I'm high right now." He sat up and straightened out as he looked over his right shoulder in the distance toward the green house. "Well J, I'll tell you this. My mom was not a good person. She didn't want me, so my dad retired. Any other questions?"

Malcom didn't want to talk about his mom. That was a soft spot with him. I assumed that was why he liked getting high so much. It wasn't about the thrill, but the emptiness of the love from a mother that left you heavy. It didn't help that his dad wasn't around much either. In a sense he was a latch key kid but with a great net worth. He dealt with his issues by smoking the pain away, and I wrote the pain away. It took a moment to realize both of us have more similarities that differences. I glanced at the sun while it took its last look at us before it departed into the clouds.

"I got the keys," Scoop said, gathering his breath.

I took the keys and searched out for which one fit. All the keys on the keychain looked like it was for doorknobs and padlocks except one. It was black and shiny and shaped as a rect-angle. It wasn't worn like the other keys, no cracks or damage. I wasn't sure if Ray had even used the cart for plowing often by the condition of it, but the key stood out to me. I put the key in the ignition, and it immediately turned on. Our loud shout of joy outdid the humming of the engine. I turned toward the bridge and moved forward slowly. Tragically, we got stuck before we could move fifty feet.

"Lower the plow, bro. You see how high it is?" Scoop intelligently spoke up.

I looked for a lever and finally found it on the dashboard. The words 'up' and 'down' gave me the answer to my problem. I lowered the plow and pressed the gas. I still couldn't move. I was stuck because of the snow from the tires. The tires were large and had plenty tread on them, but we still had to get out and dig with our hands. With our hands shaking and almost frost bitten, after five minutes we cleared a large enough path to get going and to reverse if we needed to.

With ease, the plow gathered and displaced the snow from our path. We were moving slow, but I did not want to overdo it. I looked at the cabin behind me and it started getting smaller the more I moved forward. There was a light breeze grazing the thin hairs above my lip. It sent a chill down my spine. I wasn't bothered by the cold anymore because all I could think about was the progress to real safety. I'm sure anyone would think that we were all safe in the cabin, but there was no sense of security in unknown territory.

As we approached the bridge, the plow got stuck in the snow. We were close enough to walk around and see if there was a ladder somewhere.

"All right y'all, we're stuck and we gotta find a way to get up to the street. Try to find a ladder or a way to get up to the street from the side. I know the snow is going to be high but we gotta get out of here."

I tried my best to coach the guys up. We needed to get some help as soon as we could. I started high stepping to the left side of the bridge. I didn't see a ladder, but I kept moving forward anyways. I reached the bottom of the bridge, and I looked up. The wind started blowing harder. Snow hurried off the trees and determined to invade my dreadlocks. The tips of my hair weren't black anymore. Instead, white at the tips and faded to black at the roots. I took a piece of my hair and looked straight up into the gray sky. I stuck the hair in my mouth and tasted nature's moisture. It was the earth's way of preserving me. Refilling the river of language inside of me. I thought I needed this trip to relax and get away, but I was wrong. I needed this so I could break out. Tamar's hit to my mouth was only the beginning of my journey. I turned around as I swallowed the melted snow and looked behind me. The cabin was so small. The blanket of snow glistened as the sun briefly broke out of hiding. Thoughts invaded my space as I abandoned the mission. I knew what I needed to do. My life, my experiences, my pain, my suffering, my joy, my future was all connected to my pen. I am a writer. It just took the environment for me to get it.

"Yo!" Malcom yelled at the top of his lungs. "Come help! Scoop fell in some ice!"

I rushed to the other side of the bridge. Scoop had fallen through the thin ice. I sprinted while I felt snow fall into my socks. I couldn't feel anything. I was unsure if it was because I was cold or my adrenaline. I finally reached where Scoop was. I couldn't see him splashing. He had drifted under the ice.

"Malcom, go get that rope. Tie it around me and I'll dive in."

"Nigga what?"

"Damn, just go get it hurry up!"

Malcom ran to get the rope. He fell in the snow a couple times, but eventually he made it back to me. I took the rope and tied it around my waist. I didn't know how secure the rope was, but I didn't care. If my friend was going to die, I would have died with him.

"Hold the rope and pull me up when I tug on it"

I jumped in the water. I felt the chill run through my body like electricity. I was stuck for a second, but I remembered what I needed to do. I opened my eyes and I could barely see. Just in front of me, I saw Scoop hitting the ice with his hands above him. I swam as quickly as I could. Each stroke I took became colder as I continued to rescue him. I grabbed him by his waist behind him and I tugged on the rope. I didn't feel anything pulling me back. I was nervous. I gave it two more harder tugs. Nothing. I physically screamed and tugged as hard as I could. Then, I felt the pull bringing us closer to the surface. I looked up and saw the opening. I pushed Scoop up to Malcom. He grabbed him and laid him down on the snow. It was my turn to exit the water. When Malcom reached his hand out to help me, I didn't feel my body. I was out of breath and ice formed on my ears.

I was frozen and hard like a rock. My body shook uncontrollably. I rubbed my hands together but that didn't work. If we didn't do anything quickly, I would get hypothermia. I was less worried about me when I saw Scoop's body lying there lifeless.

His once coffee-colored skin turned blue. I jumped on top of him and started doing CPR. I didn't know what I was doing. I was pushing down on his chest to get any water out of his lungs. He still didn't move. My body started to warm the more I tried to save him. I pushed slower on his chest as my emotions started to overtake me. I gave up and laid my head on his chest.

I would have to go home and catch the bus by myself. I didn't have anyone to talk to about B. My only brother was going to be gone. I didn't know if it was water from the melted snow on my hair or my tears that was falling in the water Scoop fell in. The ripples in the water formed symmetrical circles that extended as far as the opening was. The hole didn't look big enough to swallow someone whole, but it did. The snow wasn't that high over here and I saw how Scoop would have fell through.

I looked over my shoulder, and I saw Malcom running toward me with someone else with him. There was an intersection about 100 feet opposite of the bridge. I guessed that was where Scoop was trying to run toward. They reached us and the person started asking questions, but I don't remember what they were asking. All I knew was I saw an ambulance and rescue vehicles noised from afar that drew closer. When they arrived, Malcom told them about what happened and about the others in the cabin. My memory started fading as I lost consciousness. One second, I was in an ambulance with what looked like aluminum foil around me, and the next second I was in the hospital room. Finally, I was able to go to sleep.

"I made it!" I shouted. The crowd cheered. They all rushed me from the stands and lifted me above their shoulders. They carried me around the track chanting my name. James! James! James!

The chants faded. They put me down on the ground, and Tamar was standing in the distance with a trophy waiting to award me. "Baby, you did it!" She leans in to kiss me, but I float away and I'm in a room all by myself. The room is bright white, and it looks like it is never ending. A man starts walking towards me. He is tall and skinny. He is wearing all white clothing. His skin looks like brown dirt with an amber hue. He has a black beard and long black hair that isn't straight or curly. He walks straight up to me and stares at me in the face for what seems like forever. He says, "It's never the best time, but it is always the right time." I felt the urge to reach out and touch him, but as quick as I could reach out, he faded back.

"James?" A sweet-sounding voice beckoned me out of my sleep. I opened my eyes to see who it was. Tamar was at the edge of the bed in the hospital chair. I struggled to sit up because I was still exhausted.

"Hey," I whispered with a weak voice. I didn't want to say a lot because my morning breath was embarrassing.

"No, you don't have to talk. I just wanted to make sure you were all right. I wanted to tell you that you are an amazing person."

"Wait, where is Scoop?" I asked, cutting her off when I realized where I was.

"Well, he's here—" she said.

"What room number because I gotta make sure he's ok." My voice grew stronger.

"Ok, um I think you should get your rest first before you do all of that."

"Come on now! Stop playing with me. Where's Scoop?" I was so loud that the nurse came in.

"Is there a problem? Can I help you with anything, Mr. Mason?"

"Yeah, there is a problem. I need to see my friend Gary Rockland."

"I think the doctor should come and talk to you."

The nurse left the room.

"What the hell is going on? Where is my friend?"

I cried again. I grabbed the linen on the bed and squeezed as hard as I could. I took the pillow and smashed it over my face and screamed. Tamar came over to me and hugged me as I cried on her shoulder. I released everything I had from my cry through her body. Years of pain. Years of depression. Years of discouragement.

"Its ok baby. Let everything go. I'm here for you."

My body felt weak. If I was standing, I would have fallen to the ground. Tamar helped me up. Her words were short but impactful. She cried with me. At sixteen years old, I had gone through a lot and now Scoop. As I cried, the words rang in my head, *"It's never the best time, but it's always the right time."* I didn't know what that meant. All I knew was that in the current moment, Tamar was here for me, and that was all I could ask for.

"Hi, James?" The doctor came in looking for me. "Miss, can you excuse us for a minute?" Tamar walked toward the door.

"James, as soon as he's done, I'll be back, ok?" I nodded.

The doctor had the same accent as Ray did. "All right. I'm Dr. Bell. You did a mighty good thing out there. It was danger-ous, but you are a brave kid I'll tell ya. Let's talk about you first.

You do have some frost bite on your toes and fingers. I have some medication f'er ya to take for the scabs. Make sure you keep yourself warm and bundle up. You did suffer from hypothermia. Luckily enough we were able to get to you in time before it could really get to ya."

"Ok, cool. Now what about my friend Scoop?" I wasn't concerned about myself. I wanted to know the status on my brother.

Dr. Bell took a deep beath and took his glasses off. He rubbed his eyes with his left hand and sat down at the edge of the bed. His body weight lifted me slightly higher as I tensed up.

CHAPTER ELEVEN

The Next Chapter

"Winter is a bummer. Winter is the time the flowers die that we enjoy in the summer. The trees flow in the breeze, the pollen collected by bees makes us sneeze and we don't care because allergies don't make us wonder. Why do we continue to go out and explore nature? The danger of accidents, unplanned events that can make us cold as a glacier. Come winter and go quick because human nature can't handle it. The summer is the time we feel alive because the sun tells us that we need it. Death, your cold grip rips through the strongest of the elements. You've taken more than you've given please stop holding us for ransom we don't have any more sense to give. The sun lets us feel the strength of the sky as it bends through the atmosphere although the sun is further than it actually appears. Death, I know your biggest fear. You're afraid of the light. That's why you're so cold. Not cold in the sense of good but cold in the sense of bad that's why when there's light, darkness is never near. In the light you can't exist. In the light you never win. Winter. The biggest problem for you is that we will outshine you every day of the week. We see right through you. Birdseye view we fly to the South in the Winter. Animals hibernate when they see you. Nobody likes you. Well, maybe penguins and snow leopards do. We like happy feet and leopard print shoes so we still claiming them but not you, the point is. We hate you but we need you. You're not all bad. You give the earth a break from growing. You bring a beauty to the landscape of the mother. You refill the waters of the earth and give a break from mowing. We still have to shovel though. But that even builds muscle. Yes, death is destructive yet constructive. That's why it hurts so much. If God ordained it then I guess it must be good for the ecosystem. It hurts, down from family, friends, co-worker, brothers and sisters. Winter must touch every human in every region. Sometimes God lets winter hit early out of its season. But we can't choose when we can take it all in or let it all go. Listen to the creator of the seasons and He will guide you through the highs and the lows. My ode to Winter, you're not my winner. You're leashed longer than you are loosed. Tell me, when does summer come again?"

Everyone clapped for me in the church. Black suits and dresses were sprinkled over the church. I think most of them were there to make sure she was dead. I volunteered to do a poem at B's funeral because I felt so bad for what I did before I left. She didn't have much family left, so I had to step in. Her drunk of a boyfriend didn't even show up. I walked down the steps of the stage and sat right between Scoop and Tamar. They came to support me. Scoop had stopped breathing for a little bit, but the doctors were able to get him back. He was in the hospital for the week of the trip, and I was right there with him. His parents came to the hospital and made sure he was ok. The pastor was ending his eulogy and told everyone in her family to stand. I was the only one. He asked if I could stay after the service. B wanted to be cremated. It was in her will. There was no repast or burial, so after the service I went back into the pastor's office and sat down in the chair across from his desk. He had tons of books and bibles. I wondered if he had read them all or if it was for show.

"How are you dealing with this, young brother James?"

"I'm doing ok. We weren't really that close, but after her accident, I took care of her pretty well until I left for my trip. I left and she was fine. I thought her boyfriend would come and check on her while I was gone, but I was wrong. I came back and she was gone." I knew what happened, but I didn't want to explain everything to him. I knew withholding the truth wasn't good, but I wasn't lying either.

"Ok. Do you have a place to stay right now?" Pastor Glenn asked.

"Yes, I'm staying with my friend Gary Rockland and his parents. They took me in when they found out. They're going through all the paperwork to see if I can stay with them permanently."

"Oh yes!" The pastor said excited. "Brother Rockland is a member of this church. I guess I'll be seeing you more then, huh? By the way, you are extremely gifted with words. Do not let the devil take that gift from you. He already tried to do it to you before, but you persevered. God has always been with you, and he will continue to be with you. Follow him and he will direct your path.

"What I wanted to show you was some documents from Beatrice. She didn't have any other remaining family members, and it looks like you would be next in line to inherit her belongings." He cleared his throat and put his glasses on the edge of his nose and looked over them as he read a document. "It says here that you will be the owner the house when you turn eighteen unless you can have a legal guardian to sign for you. Also, you will receive the remaining balances of her bank accounts. The house is estimated to be worth $110,000, and it is paid in full. Also, she had some retirement accounts and savings that totaled up to $53,435.76."

My mouth dropped. I thought this was one of my dreams. I was never told that I was related to her. How did she get me to live with her through the foster care system? To the best of my knowledge, it didn't work out that way.

"Here's a letter she wrote a while back. The date is from October 21st, 2010. Do you want me to read it, or do you want to read it?"

"You can read it." The pastor cleared his throat and started reading.

"My dearest Grandson. James Mason Jr. I'm writing this the day after you came to my house. I can't believe I finally have you with me. I fought so hard to get you to be with me, and I finally did it. You don't know it yet, but I'm your grandmother. Your mom was so beautiful. I cry every day that the drugs got to her. When the time is right, I will have this for you with my will. You are the only family I have left. Your grandfather died right before your mom did. Early in your life, you bounced around in the foster care system until I was able to set things right. I know you may

not understand what I am about to tell you now, but when you get older, it will all make sense. Your grandfather is not your real grandfather. I got drunk one night and I slept with some Black man. Thank goodness your mom could pass for white. I raised her to be white, but her black side couldn't stay down. She loved your dad, and I didn't. I know it's hard to understand but that's just the way things were. Well, your dad got in trouble because he was hanging out with the wrong crowd, and I didn't want Patrice to be around that crowd. What I did was try to protect her. I had her father set him up to go away for a long time. Little did I know that she was pregnant with you. I didn't want her to make the same mistake that I did, but it was too late. My husband died shortly after you were born and that is when your mom got hooked on the same drugs that got your dad in jail. Everything is my fault, and this is my way of making it right. You have the Lewis blood in you so I will make sure you know what it means to be a part of this family. My methods may be different, but you will thank me when I'm gone. You're still a Lewis."

I didn't know how to react to the news. I felt like I was in an episode of *Black Mirror*. I leaned back in the chair to contemplate what was said to me. Pastor Glenn was talking, but I didn't listen to what he was saying. I was in my own thoughts. I started to imagine my life if I had known B was my grandmother. Could I have made a bigger impact on her life to stop drinking? Could I have listened a little more? Since she knew this information, why didn't she tell me? Why didn't my dad write me and tell me about her? I had so many questions that were unanswered. Nonetheless, I needed to move on. What would be the next chapter of my life? What do I do next? These were all questions that I needed to investigate.

Shortly after Pastor Glenn read the letter, we finished up and I met Scoop and Tamar in front of the church. It had been a month since the trip to the Northern Lights. I walked toward them with my hands in my pockets. Scoop leaned over and whispered something to Tamar that made her laugh.

"What's so funny?" I asked. "We did just leave a funeral you know. We shouldn't be laughing."

"All I said was watch him come out lying talking about B left him some money because you were walking with your hands in your pockets," Scoop said jokingly.

I looked deviously at them both and said, "Actually, B was my grandma. I was her only family left, and I got all her bank accounts and the house." They were just as shocked as I was. They congratulated me as if I had won the lottery. Isaiah pulled to the front of the church to pick us we. I was staying at Scoop's house since we came back from Alaska.

We got in big trouble after everything was settled. We had to write letters to the review board of the school and explain why we should remain enrolled at South Shore. After individual reviews and meetings, we were suspended for the rest of the year and had to do community service. Malcolm got the grunt of the punishment because he placed all the blame on himself. He was able to get rid of all the marijuana that was on him. I felt bad for Isaiah and Tamar because they had never been in trouble like that before. We would all start our Junior year on probation the following school year. Malcom was moving to Florida because his dad took a coaching job at a college.

Me, Isaiah, Scoop, and Tamar went to my house to get the rest of my things. Mr. Rockland was determined to adopt me so me and Scoop can be real brothers. I walked into B's room to see what else she had. It was a faint smell of smoke and alcohol. The worn brown paint on the wall had sprinkles of mold spots throughout. There were boxes of cigarettes and empty beer bottles in her closet and under her bed. When she was alive, I never went into her room to clean. This was my first time in there. I flipped the mattress to see what was underneath, and there were hundreds of unopened letters. I threw the mattress off the frame and collected them. There were so many that they all couldn't fit in my hands. A few letters fell to the floor at the same time, Tamar knocked on the door and entered. She picked up the remaining letters that fell.

"What are these?" she asked.

"I don't know. I found these under the mattress. I didn't even have a chance to look at them."

I sat on floor and leaned against the dresser. I dropped the stacks of letters between my legs. I felt the matted, grayish carpet between my fingers. I started to run my hand back and forth while crumbs ran across my knuckles. I grew courage to look at the address. It was from inmate 72786-953, James Mason Sr., Waupun Correctional Institution. I flipped the letters around and saw that they were all from my dad. I had never met my dad, at least from what I could remember, but these letters gave me a better understanding of his image. I started to weep as I read the letters from him. Years' worth of letters overwhelmed me. Tamar slid next to me and held my head up on her shoulder. He told me everything about B, and how she hated him. He told me about he didn't do what he was convicted of. He told me about my mom, and how beautiful she was. He told me that he was going to get out soon to come and get me. I believed everything he said. The letters were funny, well written, and compassionate. The last letter he sent was two weeks before we went to the Northern Light trip. It was the one that broke me. He apologized for not being there for me and my mom. He hoped that I would come visit him one day because he hasn't seen me since I was five. The only reason he knew where I lived was because B wanted to torture him with unsent letters back to him. At least that's what he said.

"Hey," Tamar interjected as I was reading, "I think you've read enough for one day. We can pick back up tomorrow, ok?"

"Yeah, I guess so."

I was overwhelmed and that was a great idea. Tamar, sitting next to me thumbing through the letters, grabbed me and held on to my head. I heard her heartbeat as she breathed. She stroked my locs and told me everything will be all right. I embraced her back, and I finally released everything. Years of not knowing and abuse finally subsided. B was gone, I have a chance to see my dad, and I could get real information about my mom. We sat on the floor for thirty minutes until we finished cleaning out everything I wanted in the room.

After everything was cleared out, Scoop and I bid our goodbyes to Tamar and Isaiah. We went to his house and stayed in his room. It was cramped, but I was able to make a pallet on the floor until they could clear out the extra room they had for me. Scoop and I talked about my dad and the letters I found.

"Yo, we should go visit your dad, bro. I think it'll be good for both of you."

"Yeah, I want to go soon. Maybe your dad can take us."

"Ok, I'll call him in here so we can talk about it. Hey dad, can you come in here for a minute please?"

"What is it, son?" Mr. Rockland asked.

"So, J found some letters from his dad at his house, and he wanted to go visit him soon. You think you can take him?"

"Of course. Where is he at?"

I handed him a letter.

"Wait, James is you're father?" Mr. Rockland was taken aback when he found out the news.

"Yeah," I responded confused. "Scoop, do you have that picture from the camera?"

Scoop handed the picture to his dad, and his mouth gaped open.

"You do not understand how much I missed this guy. I regret not reconnecting with him. That was my guy, my brother. We were inseparable. I didn't realize that he had a kid with Patrice. I didn't even think to connect the dots."

"I have other letters too. He said that he wasn't involved with drugs, and he didn't have them on him when he was pulled over. B left me a letter about what really happened. I don't know if you can do anything about it, but could we possibly investigate that?" I asked.

"I'm on it right now."

He left the room and went on the phone to talk to the right people. Everything felt so surreal. All these experiences and setbacks put me into the position I'm in now. I realized that I wouldn't change what I've been through for anything. Experiences will only make my writing that much better. I decided that I would write until I could get a collection of my poems and stories published. Maybe a novel or autobiography too. I told Scoop my goals and dreams. I showed him my book of writings and poems.

"Bro, you need a producer? Because these are bars! Your cadence may be a little off, but I can manage," Scoop said laughing. "But in all seriousness, what's next for you? There is a talent show that you should sign up for at The Flex downtown. You should go."

"You think I'm good enough to go?" I asked.

"Yes. Just get to work. You got about a week to get ready." I was hesitant, but I decided to do it. I wanted to go visit my dad before I did anything.

The next day, Scoop and I went to his dad to see if he could take me go do see him. He agreed and signed us up on the visitors list go see him that upcoming weekend. I was nervous as the days went on. I didn't know what I was going to say or how I was going to react. All I knew was I was going to cry. I was turning into a water head. I talked with Tamar about the trip over the phone, and she was excited for me. She couldn't come with me because she had a softball tournament that weekend.

The week flew by, and Saturday arrived. It was a two-hour drive to get to the prison. To pass the time, I brought my notebooks full of writings to get some ideas down for the talent show. The drive was too bumpy for me to write how I wanted to, so I decided to brainstorm. After the long drive, we arrived at the facility.

We walked to the front and was greeted by an officer. Scoop and I looked at each other and gazed at all the metal and barbed wire on the building. Even though it was 75° degrees outside, the grounds felt cold. We walked in and checked in with the other visitors at the front desk. I was so amazed at what prison looked like. It felt like the basement at B's. In the waiting room, we sat and waited to be called in. Being in a room full of families and friends waiting to see their loved ones was heartbreaking to see. The loud buzzer sounded and the gate opened.

One by one, each inmate walked, then an officer unshackled their hands so they could go see their visitors. My dad finally entered the room and looked around. We didn't let him know we were coming. All he knew was he had visitors today. I don't know if he ever had any visitors. I saw him look around and finally lock eyes with me. My stomach dropped as I walked toward the table with Scoop and Mr. Rockland. I wanted to run into his arms like a little boy who saw his father come home from work after a long day. I restrained myself. The closer we came to each other, the more we prepared for an embrace. At last, the hug from my father was the greatest joy I had ever felt. His patchy beard scratched the side of my cheek. The mild smell of detergent seeped from his jumpsuit filled my nostrils. He hugged me with compassion and love. I felt the eyes of the guards taunt me but I ignored them. The ten-second hug felt like a lifetime. We sat down and no one said anything because we knew that we were saturated in that moment.

"Naw, that can't be you! G-Rock?" my dad asked, wiping tear from his eyes.

"Come on bro, you know who it is. How you been, big dog?"

"Yo, it's been how long since we last talked? I was getting transferred so many times, I didn't even want to reach out to anybody because by the time I got word back I would have been gone. But before I got locked up you went to the military and went ghost on me," my dad joked.

"Don't do me like that, man. You know what it is."

"I'm messing with you, bro. Is this your boy here?"

"Yep. That's my oldest Gary III but we call him Scoop. Him and your boy are best friends. How crazy is that?"

"How are you, sir. It's nice to meet you." Gary said respectfully. I've never seen Scoop so formal before.

"Likewise, but don't call me sir. I'm not that old, kid." My dad paused and looked at me and shook his head in disbelief. "Wow. I can't believe you're here. I thought I would never talk to you again let alone see you. How did you get my information? That old racist let you come see me?"

"No, she died a few weeks ago, and I found all the letters you sent."

"I knew she was doing that. That lady always had it out for me. She didn't like that your mom was mixed. That confuses me because she must have been drunk to sleep with a Black guy because when I tell you she was as mean as she could get. Well, son, I'm just glad you're here right now. We got so much catching up to do in such a short amount of time."

"Yeah," I responded. "We do have some catching up because there may be a way you can get out of here. In a letter that B wrote, she admitted that she had set you up. Mr. Rockland said that he would make all the right calls to get you out of here and get your record expunged."

"Now, I said we got catching up to do son. Not lying."

Mr. Rockland interrupted, "No, he's right J-Man. I have a lawyer working on it now. We should be coming up here soon to get more information from you. We have a legit shot. It sounds too good to be true, but you may not have to wait until 2026 to get out."

My dad covered his face with his hands and started to cry.

"Hands inmate!" One officer yelled at him.

He looked as if all the shame of being in prison was finally coming off him. I couldn't imagine all the trauma and problems that he suffered while being in a cell with hundreds of other men. Day in and day out smelling the same rotten smell that became normal. Disgusting food that turned into gourmet meals. Having the luxury of being out in the yard supervised for short periods of time turned into heaven. I wouldn't wish this on anyone.

We all talked and caught up until the time was up. I didn't want to go. I wanted to bring my daddy with me to the house. I didn't tell him about the house or the money because I wanted to surprise him once he gets his record clear. I thought it was important for me to take care of him after he got out until he could get back on his feet. We left, but not before one final embrace. I pulled back from him, and I saw the handsome face behind the rough jail look that grabbed him. We scheduled weekly visits so I could show him my writing skills and everything else that I was interested in. It was a breath of fresh air. When we finally reached back to the house, I sat on the floor with my pen in one hand and my notebook in the other because I got my motivation to write for the talent show.

May 24th Freedom

What do you call a prisoner who served his time? What do you call a person who decided to follow his own mind? What do you call a people who decided that this is it? What do you call a patient who took their last chemo trip? Who do you call on when you see that you're stuck? Who do you call on when you're stuck in never enough? Who do you call when you're confined to one space? Who do you call when you no longer want to be restrained? F.R.E.E.D.O.M. Identified as the ability to act or change without constraint. One is free if it can change easily and is not constrained in its present state. Forget what you've learned and unlearn the past. Ready yourself for the future because hard times doesn't last. Edify your mind and become your whole self. Evaluate your emotions because they're one thing, and the next they're something else. Discipline your actions to be intentional and concise. Overstand your surrounding because being under isn't nice. Motivate yourself into staying in control. F.R.E.E.D.O.M isn't a physical position it's a state of mind. They can have the body, but the soul is mine. Take up control and lay down oppression. Moving in and out of state of mind should be done in discretion. When bound encounters free, they say free is bound. Because free isn't moved by what society deems allowed. Bound is depressing, it's like staring at a brick wall out of a window, while being blind. You think you have a great view but the truth is everybody knows it but you. Release from the confines of 'this is what I should be based on this.' Free is excellent and bound is below average. Being free will cost you nothing out of pocket but it is never cheap. The next question you should ask is HOW much does it cost for me to be free.

When I wrote down the last word, Scoop's mom yelled out, "James, come down so I can retwist your hair." I then whispered under my breath,

"FREEDOM."